**IT WAS THE OPPORTUNITY JULIO
HAD DREAMED OF...
AND HE WAS SURE HE WAS GOING TO BLOW IT.**

The announcer paused and studied a piece of paper he was holding. "The first song," he said, "is entitled 'Life Continues All the Same.' The words and music are by Julio Iglesias, and the composer himself will sing the song."

The announcer stepped back and the audience began to applaud, but Julio just stood there.

"Go ahead," Enrique urged, "you're on."

Julio still couldn't move. A minute passed, and the announcer looked over. Enrique motioned for him to be patient, then turned to Julio.

"You can't do this, Julio. You can't back out now."

"I won't," he said, his voice barely above a whisper. "I just need a minute. That's all, just a minute."

"You've already taken a minute!" Enrique squealed. "What do you want, another one?"

"Yes," Julio said, "just one more."

Exasperated, Enrique pursed his lips and stepping behind Julio, literally pushed him onto the stage.

That day, a legend was born.

JULIO!

Jeff Rovin

BANTAM BOOKS
TORONTO · NEW YORK · LONDON · SYDNEY · AUCKLAND

JULIO!

A Bantam Book / September 1985

ISBN 0-553- 25439-1

Published simultaneously in the United States and Canada

Bantam Books are published by Bantam Books, Inc. Its trade-
mark, consisting of the words "Bantam Books" and the por-
trayal of a rooster, is Registered in U.S. Patent and Trademark
Office and in other countries. Marca Registrada. Bantam
Books, Inc., 666 Fifth Avenue, New York, New York 10103.

PRINTED IN THE UNITED STATES OF AMERICA

H   0 9 8 7 6 5 4 3 2 1

ACKNOWLEDGMENTS

The author is indebted to Marlene Schweitzer, who patiently and meticulously translated countless magazines, newspapers, and documents from the Spanish; and to Alice Grover for translating a lesser, but no less valuable, stack of material from the French.

Thanks as well go to Josue R. Rivas of the newspaper *El Diario-La Prensa;* Julio Yanez in Barcelona; Vincent Mahiques of Roig Spanish Books in New York City; Ray and Diana Harryhausen in London; the archivists at the Lincoln Center music library; Felipe Floresca of U.S. Hispanic Affairs; the staff of the French and Spanish Book Corp.; Joe Kelleher and the very cooperative people at Coca-Cola; and to research assistant Bob Sodaro. Deep thanks also, as ever, to editor Deb Futter, and to Jim Trupin.

When I say I love you, no matter how short-lived, I say it with all my heart.

—Julio Iglesias

PROLOGUE

Julio Iglesias wasn't an irresponsible young man, yet what he did on that warm September night was not far short of sheer insanity.

Just a few days shy of his twentieth birthday, Julio was a person whom others found to be intense beyond his years, far less reckless and frivolous than most people his age. His unusual sense of responsibility grew from having three important goals in life, any two of which would have constituted a full-time job for a less driven individual. In no particular order of importance, Julio's ambitions were to graduate from law school and join the diplomatic corps; to become a semiprofessional soccer goalie, a dream he'd nurtured since childhood; and to fall in love with as many women as humanly possible—two a day, if he could have his way.

All of these pursuits were very serious to Julio, and his rigid devotion to them is one reason he let himself go a little mad that night at Majadahonda, a small town outside of Madrid.

Julio had spent the entire day at an annual *feria*, an open-air festival. He and his friends Tito Arroyo, Enrique Clemente, and Pedro Luis Iglesias (no relation) had exhausted themselves sampling the food and chasing the girls, dancing with them and stealing kisses on the cheek, showing the ladies how brave and agile they were by chasing the cows and taunting the small bulls that meandered through the plaza.

Despite all the gallavanting, none of the boys had had anything to drink that day. Indeed, to Julio, having control and being alert were so important that he rarely drank at all. He would nurse a glass of wine or a beer now and then, just to be sociable, but when he sat at an outdoor café with friends or stood studying the girls at a party, Julio preferred to have a soft drink in his hand. The nineteen-year-old actually had very few vices. Alone, he would occasionally light up a cigarette, rarely finishing it, and he never smoked anything stronger than tobacco. Nor was he any fonder of drugs than he was of alcohol, wanting nothing in his system that would impair his judgment or make it impossible for him to study the girls. In fact, the high he got from being with women, even just watching them, was far greater than any high he could possibly get from chemicals.

It was nearly two A.M., after most of the girls had left, when Julio and his friends decided to head back to Madrid. Though it had been a full day, Julio left reluctantly; he still had a bit of fire left in him and, as the boys packed into his red sportscar, he flicked on the radio, drumming on the steering wheel as they drove off.

The route carried the boys through scenic countryside, along narrow roads which wound through lovely woods. Still keyed-up and a little giddy from the lateness of the hour, Julio accelerated as they entered a gravel stretch of roadway. It was a chance to open up, to spite life by going faster than the rules said he should. Julio seized the opportunity, the car leaving a thin, serpentine trail of smoke as he pushed it through one curve after another.

Julio's passengers all laughed at first, but as he climbed toward forty miles an hour, Tito began to get uneasy. The road was damp and the curves were sharp. His eyes shifted from the road to his friends.

Seated in the back beside Pedro, Tito shouted over the music, "Julio, be careful!"

Julio smiled, his fingers tapping out the beat. "Don't worry," he replied, and playfully pressed on the accelerator. The car shot from forty to fifty miles an hour.

Tito glanced anxiously at the speedometer and watched as it edged toward sixty. "Come on, Julio, that's enough. Put the brake on—just a little."

Julio stole a quick glance into the car. He could vaguely see the other two, and they didn't appear as nervous as Tito. Surely they understood that this was good for them—to go fast for a change. To be free. Grinning, Julio pushed the car past sixty, then seventy, on roads where half that speed was considered dangerous.

Speed. Nothing came fast enough for Julio Iglesias. Life demanded that everything be done a step at a time, and that frustrated him. He didn't particularly like school, and wished that he could snap his fingers and be done with it, get out of the classroom and see some of the world. He wished that he didn't have to spend so much time standing idle at the soccer net while his opponents worked the ball toward him. He wanted them to smack ball after ball in his direction, let him stop it time after time and bask in the cheers of the crowd. He wished that he didn't have to bother courting girls, putting up with the dancing and the kissing on the cheek. What he wanted to do was make love to every girl with whom he fell in love—which, as it happened, was most of the girls he met. But he couldn't tear through life, and so on that late summer night Julio Iglesias tore through the tortuous roads leading to Madrid.

All four boys saw the signpost warning of a curve up ahead, but Julio ignored it. Gripping the handle of the door with one hand, Tito lay the other on Julio's shoulder. "Don't, Julio. Don't do this. That's a dangerous curve ahead."

"Don't worry," Julio repeated, a trifle annoyed, his foot sinking on the pedal. The car cracked one hundred miles an hour, smoke spewing behind it in a thick cloud. He was no longer moving to the music but had settled back in his seat, braced against the wheel and concentrating on the road. He barely saw the other two markers as they flashed briefly in his lights, alerting him to the upcoming curve.

By this time, the car's occupants had all fallen still and silent. Though Julio's little adventure had ceased to be fun, they decided not to say anything critical of him. They knew that Julio thrived on challenge, on a dare, and they didn't want to say anything that might encourage their compadre to speed up. They simply sat back and hoped for the best.

For his part, Julio was utterly unconcerned. He had driven the road before, many times, and while he had never gone this fast, he was a very good driver. He knew about the turn just ahead, the one ominously nicknamed Death Curve, and he felt he could take it. But when he finally sped into it, he realized that he was in trouble. He hadn't remembered the curve having quite the horseshoe twist that it did, and as he shot into it he saw at once that he wouldn't be able to hold the road.

Cutting the wheel hard to the left, Julio jammed on the brake. All of the occupants screamed as the sportscar's momentum turned it round and round like a top, toward the incline; the sickening pirouette ended abruptly only when the vehicle skidded down a short bank and slammed into a tree, snapping into two pieces. Remarkably, even as the two twisted chunks settled on their side, the car's bright headlights still blazed, throwing light up into the trees, while the radio incongruously piped lively music into the night.

Now, of course, Julio Iglesias was not hopping in his seat. Wincing, his chest and back filled with pain, he managed to move slightly. But he promptly forgot his own agony: whatever he may have just done to *his* body, Julio prayed that his wild indulgence had not been responsible for the deaths of three other human beings.

CHAPTER ONE

When a man has transcended all traditional measures of popularity and wealth, when he has conquered more countries than any soldier ever dreamed of winning, it is only natural that the line between fact and fantasy begins to blur. Not only in the adoring eye of the public, but in the mind of the man himself.

The seeds for this attitude were sown during the painful years of rehabilitation which followed the car accident. Slowly, this very physical young man, this athlete on the soccer field and in the bedroom, metamorphosed into a very metaphysical young man. In Julio's way of looking at things, every event has a metaphorical side. Since the singer doesn't read, and doesn't enjoy watching TV, when he is alone he broods— searching for meaning, softening his often violent gut reaction to things by finding a softer, philosophical side.

For example, in 1981, Julio was relaxing at his estate in Indian Creek, Florida, when he heard shouts for assistance. Running outside, Julio found two of his Rolls-Royces burning. The automobiles had been protected under plastic covers which, baked by the hot sun, had simply begun to burn. Julio loved the cars very much, literally having a sensual attachment to them: he liked nothing more than to climb barefoot into the vehicles and let his feet caress the pedals as he drove.

Staring at the flames, Julio did not want to see anyone hurt trying to extinguish the blaze, and ordered everybody back. Amid apologies from his house staff, which he quietly assured them were unnecessary, Julio stood watching the fire. He was upset, yet even as he stood there mourning the loss, he felt a sense of relief. He could replace the cars, but that thought wasn't what had calmed him. Their destruction reminded Julio that while he may have conquered the world, he was not its master. "I cannot have everything," he would later admit. "I *should* not have everything. Perhaps," he even realized, "I do not *want* to have everything."

That wasn't quite true. He wanted very desperately to have his three children living with him instead of with their mother, and he wanted to become a superstar in the United States, where he was still a virtual unknown. What Julio no longer wanted was every *material* thing. So much of his life had been filled with, in his words, the effort "to acquire things." The fire underscored the fact that that was no way to live. Jamming his hands in his pockets and strolling back into the house, pausing to sniff one of the blue roses in the garden, he told himself that life "is much more than having two spendid autos, perhaps the best in the world, in my garage."

Today, two of his most important possessions keep that thought ever-fresh in his mind: they are the sole survivors of the blaze, the license plates of one car and the hood ornament (he calls it his Oscar) of the other.

"They are there in the billiard parlor," he says, "near the gold records, near my caricatures, near the books, the pictures, the honors, and all sorts of things like that." He enjoys looking at them for they remind him that his legacy to the world must be more than an estate and cars and possessions. What matters is his music.

In light of Julio's pensive, almost poetic (if gentrified) view of the world, it was only natural that, in time, he would begin to ascribe symbolic significance to past events in his own life—starting with his birth.

Julio was born into a very well-to-do family. His father, Julio Iglesias Puga, was a prominent gynecologist ("the stork's pastor," as his son refers to him) whose roots in Galicia, in the northwest of Spain, Julio considers his own. The song *Un Canto a Galicia,* one of the earliest written and sung by the future superstar, is a proud salute to the province. The doctor's wife, Rosario de la Cueva, came from Madrid but had a mixed ancestry, her forebears having come from Puerto Rico, Cuba, and Andalusia.

When Julio was born, the couple was living very comfortably in Madrid's Arguelles district, an upper-middle-class part of town not far from the lovely Parque del Oeste. The baby was delivered in a modern hospital in Madrid on September 23, 1943. The birth was far from routine. After a long labor, Rosario was not sufficiently dilated to deliver—*"del tamaño de un duro,"* as her condition was informally known, "as big as a duro." A duro is a small coin, an opening hardly sufficient to allow for a normal birth.

At the time, cesarean deliveries were neither as routine nor as safe as they are today, and there was great reluctance to perform one. While the doctors waited to see what would happen, a priest was called in

case either the mother or the child required one. All
the while, Dr. Iglesias paced in a far corner of the
room, waiting to see what happened. He knew that if
he gave the okay for a cesarean, Rosario might die. Nor
was there any guarantee that the operation would save
the baby.

There was also talk of inserting a large needle into
the birth canal and poking the top of the baby's head, a
practice sometimes used to stir reluctant babies into a
state of activity. Dr. Iglesias knew that the procedure
should be tried, but some impulse made him decide
against it; a fortuitous decision, as it turned out. The
baby happened to be lying face first ("looking at the
world," as Julio describes it), and had the needle been
inserted, it would not have pricked the skull but would
have scarred or possibly blinded the child.

Dr. Iglesias waited while Rosario struggled through
her labor. According to Julio, that was when he sent
them a "sign" that he would not only live but pros-
per: he says that he literally cried out from the
womb, just as Napoleon was reported to have done.
What this means, he explains, is that such children
"become beings of privilege, even though they also
become, through time, beings of solitude—a ques-
tionable honor."

Since crying in the womb is equivalent to crying
underwater, it is clear that either Julio or his parents
have attempted to mythologize his birth. Regardless,
shortly after Julio's brief communique, his father said
succinctly from the other side of the room, "Cut open
the mother."

Drying the blood and swabbing her with vinegar-
saturated cotton, the doctors performed the cesarean.
Fortunately, both mother and son survived—though

Rosario says she still feels the pain of the operation whenever the seasons change.

As soon as she learned that it was a son she had borne by cesarean, Rosario said, "Caesar—he will be called Julio Caesar." But the boy's father disapproved, no doubt aware of how Julius Caesar ended up. Instead, they named the small, black-haired child Julio José.

Julio entered the Iglesias household with what he perceives to have been a pair of strikes against him. First, he says, "I was born by chance . . . pure circumstance, an accident." He also had to overcome his mother's long-standing wish that her firstborn be a girl. "I do not know if this caused a trauma, a deep one, within me," he admits, but he was certainly aware of Rosario's preference and today, though it's his mother who stays with him in Indian Creek, Julio speaks of his father with a deeper affection than he ever musters for Rosario. That isn't just the result of the misogyny which was a natural part of European life at the time; it is hero worship. Julio senior was articulate, intense, strong, and very much in control of himself; because he was a doctor, everyone looked up to him and treated him with great respect. He made Julio proud, and it was enough for Julio just to be in the elder Iglesias's presence, watching him study or talk with other adults, and especially going with him to the soccer stadium. "Pity that children grow up," he says and grins. "I feel content, which is not very frequent for me, remembering those times— my father and I going to see soccer games. Always with my father. . . ." he says wistfully.

"For my mother," Julio continues, "I have the typical love that a child has for his mother"—but that is faint praise indeed. In fairness to Rosario, while it was her husband who took their son to soccer games it was she, being home all the time, who was responsible for discipline. And while she didn't realize it at the time, the kind of punishment she devised for Julio—locking him in the closet or bathroom—left a very serious scar on the boy.

Actually, because Julio was an extremely sensitive, very impressionable child, everything that happened to him, the mundane as well as the traumatic, left vivid fingerprints all over his psyche. For example, Julio's oldest memory is of the blue ceramic tiles on the porch in his house; today, the singer's favorite color is blue. As a toddler, he used to run away from the maid when they went for a walk; today, Julio is still an impulsive, restless soul.

Much of what the impressionable Julio experienced as a child proved beneficial to him, especially his early exposure to soccer—in particular, to the legendary goalie Ricardo Zamora. Today, Julio gushingly describes Zamora as "the greatest goalkeeper of all time, not only in the history of Spanish sports, but perhaps in the history of the world." Hyperbole or not, Julio believed it, and the perfection Zamora represented became Julio's personal Holy Grail: he pursued that level of excellence during the fourteen years he played soccer and, when he was forced to give it up, he sought perfection in the women he dated, the songs he recorded, and even in the way he handled an automobile. No ball got past Zamora on the field; Julio meant for nothing to get past him in life.

The young boy first got to play soccer competitively during his second year at Colegio de los Sagrados Corazónes—the School of the Holy Hearts, a Roman Catholic school which he entered when he was four years old. As it turned out, apart from his sterling soccer career, Julio would achieve nothing else of distinction at the school. In fact, his lack of academic accomplishment was something of an embarrassment to his parents.

Julio wasn't a lazy child; quite the contrary, he had an abundance of energy and enthusiasm. But, then as now, he had energy only for those things which interested him. "My best marks were in literature and in art," he recalls, "and very poor in math. The worst. The aesthetic moves me; the poetic, the lyric, the thoughtful. Not so with math or science."

As much as the arts may have "moved" him, nothing interested young Julio quite so much as being the center attraction, both on the soccer field and in the classroom. When it came to soccer, Julio freely admits that even had he not idolized Zamora and posted the star's pictures on his bedroom walls, he never could have been anything but a goalie. It was a star position roughly equivalent to a quarterback in football or a pitcher in baseball, and that appealed to him. Though Julio quickly learned that goalkeeping wasn't nirvana—there were long, boring stretches when the ball was elsewhere on the field—the idea of being the only obstacle between an adversary and the goal challenged him. It demanded perfection, allowed for no mistakes. Goalkeeping afforded two other rewards as well: it meant that people would watch his every move, which excited him; and, like the delicious feel of the automobile pedal against his bare foot, Julio says he found nothing to compare with the tactile aspect of being a goalie, "to take the ball in my hands ... to possess" (which, he acknowledges with a knowing smile, "is something to be studied" by a qualified Freudian).

Contrary to his noble endeavors on the playing field, Julio describes himself as having been "full of mischief, and at times intolerable" in the classroom.

The floggings handed out as a matter of course at the school and the more unpleasant punishment which awaited him at home didn't stop him.

"I had no bad intentions," Julio goes on. "I don't think that there is any child that really has bad intentions. What happened is that I was a lot like Don Quixote. I was more active than passive and I liked to find and discover new things. Books and desks did not tie me down. The intellectual has never been my strong point; I have never wanted to find guidance in what someone else has to say."

In retrospect, it's clear that the most serious cause of Julio's misadventures was not boredom or his natural impatience but, again, his "exhibitionist" nature, the need "to be different, to have people take notice of me." On the soccer field, he could accomplish that by deed. In the real world, though, he felt that he was unattractive and that no one would notice him if he *didn't* act up. "I was almost a midget in size," he complains, "and I had hair like a porcupine: black and unmanageable. I fought a daily battle with it. I broke combs. I applied tons of water. But inevitably, the hair returned to its place, going forward. I looked pitiful, but I did my best to transcend this."

Julio's lack of self-esteem was further heightened by the arrival of his only sibling, younger brother Carlos who, from the start, was always considered the good-looking one in the family.

Prophetically, Julio says that it was especially important to him that he be noticed and liked by girls. Girls brought beauty and tranquility into his frenetic world, and Julio found these qualities appealing. Of course, getting noticed by girls was one thing; any hyperactive child could do that. Getting them to like him, though, was quite another. And as a youngster, neither he nor his friends had quite mastered that art. Julio was able to get his way with boys by bullying them, whether it was dividing up the teams for soccer or assigning field positions. "Let Julito do it!" became something of a byword among his companions, according to Julio. "Julito will take care of everything!" they knew. But "Julito" couldn't force girls to like him. They had to be finessed, he discovered, taken for a walk or given gifts. And even then they were fickle, something which frustrated him from the start.

Julio's first experience with the hurt of love occurred when he fell for María. María had blond hair, light-colored eyes, and fair skin, and all of the boys adored and courted her. Thus, whenever she flirted with a boy, especially one who was older, the rest of them would suffer pain that, in Julio's words, was "stupendous and horrible." So great was Julio's love for María that it actually inspired him to write his first lines of verse, a love poem which, alas, he did not keep. In his own poetic way of looking at things, though, Julio doesn't consider the poem lost but simply to have "died"—just like his love for María died when he eventually turned his attention to other young ladies.

Julio's home life was generally a pleasant one. When he wasn't playing soccer or watching it or reading about it in the newspaper, he was usually out riding his bicycle. As a very young child, he was particularly fond of tearing through the streets on a tricycle that looked like a motorcycle—riding fast, of course, faster than the other children on the block. He also spent a lot of time at the movies. His mother was a movie fanatic and, as Julio senior frequently worked long hours, young Julio was his mother's frequent escort.

When Julio was alone at night or on rainy days, he spent a lot of time reading comic books. Though he was not a collector, and has no hobbies to this day, comic books were something that he hoarded. To his credit, Julio's taste was eclectic: he read everything from sports comics to the adventures of the American FBI. "I would read them week after week," he says, smiling, "and they were the only books in my library"—the only books save for his schoolbooks, which he says "remained at the bottom" of a drawer from the time he came home each day until the following morning.

But despite his joys and disappointments, nothing in Julio's young life affected him quite so deeply as being what he describes as "a prisoner in the closet." Julio says, "I am terrorized by the lack of physical liberty, much more than intellectual liberty." The latter, he says, "just dulls your five senses"; imprisonment, on the other hand, restricts movement, which is "the worst punishment that can be inflicted on me."

When he was locked up, Julio would sit down and, in his words, "think and think and think. And fantasize." Anything to keep his mind off his predicament. He would dream about receiving a standing ovation on the soccer field, or about "girls and their smiles and going arm in arm for a walk." He would run through the stories in his comic books, and imagine being one of the heroes. But, after a half hour or so, "even though dreaming is endless, and without a chain attached to it," Julio says he simply wasn't able to concentrate any more. And when that happened, he found it difficult to breathe and "would start to scream like crazy." He'd call for his mother, beg her to open the door, cry that he was suffocating, that he was dying, that he'd learned his lesson. He describes his shouts as "pathetic," and when Rosario would finally come and let him out, he'd rush past her, his face dirty and covered with tears, and stumble onto the balcony where he'd stand for long minutes gulping down air. It was a common enough form of discipline among Spanish families at the time, though that was no consolation to Julio.

To this day, Julio retains "an obsession about lacking physical liberty," a fact which made the car accident and his subsequent paralysis all the more ironic—and unbearable.

CHAPTER TWO

Not surprisingly, the time of year Julio liked the best was the summer. School was out, punishments were rare, and he got to do the two things he liked the best: be active outside and spend time with his father.

To young Julio, the approach of summer was made official not by the longer hours and the warming sun, but by a change in the priests at the school. They seemed to lighten up a bit, and would always give Julio the singular honor of joining them and their colleagues from other regions in a very competitive game of soccer. "We would play alone," Julio remembers fondly, "just the priests and myself," with Julio as goalie—and not just because he *wanted* that position. "I was, permit me to say this in modesty—yet at the same time with pride—the best goalkeeper in the history of my school." And a good thing, too, since, he says, "they would really hit me . . . I don't know whether with bad intentions or not." He shrugs. Malice or not, he had a wonderful time and cut quite a figure on the field: small and dark, his hair tumbling this way and that, he darted from post to post as the priests in their dark, ankle-length robes tried to boot the ball past him. It was almost worth the year of suffering to be able to meet the priests as an equal.

The Iglesias family traditionally spent the summer in Peniscola, where in Julio's words they were "an institution." During these active months, Julio would dress in his sailor suit and sandals and spend a lot of time on his bicycle. Not only did bicycling provide him with an outlet for his energy, it allowed him to show off and fed his ego: "I had equilibrium," he says. "I was a magician, an authentic 'Bahamontes,' the best in the circus." So obvious was Julio's desire to be applauded that adults made a point of telling him not that they enjoyed his wheelies or hands-off riding, but that they took their vacations there solely "to see the son of Dr. Iglesias riding a bike."

The rest of the time Julio was busy at the beach, where he would constantly try to best his time for juggling a soccer ball, keeping it from touching the ground by bouncing it from his toe to his head (he'd usually stop after an hour, though he could have gone on longer). When his head could no longer take the pounding, Julio would make a mark on the ground, step back, and kick the ball precisely on the spot. When Carlos or a friend weren't around to return the ball, Julio would entertain himself by hopping on his hands and seeing if he could beat his previous time for doing a handstand. Competing with others wasn't a requisite with Julio: he was quite content to compete with himself.

However, in one area he was very competitive, and that was in seeing whether he or his brother had grown the most during the summer. The only reason he didn't kick about going home after vacation was because on his return he could put his back against the wall and have his mother mark off his height. As one of the genuine highlights of his youth, he cites the year that he came back and found that he had grown a full nine centimeters in two months. Not only did he beat the pants off Carlos, but he felt he had *caused* the growth to take place: he'd exercised more than ever before, making himself so hungry that he literally ate on the extra height.

For his part, sweet, quiet Carlos enjoyed the measuring, too, though not so he could beat his older brother. He didn't yearn to beat Julio in anything. Even when they fought, Carlos would only lash out at his brother as a last, desperate resort, after Julio had struck first, and hard. Rather, Carlos liked the measuring because he enjoyed being a part of anything that Julio did. (Fortunately for the older boy's psyche, when Carlos finally did achieve physical parity as a teenager, Julio was old enough to realize that genetics, at least, were beyond his ability to control.)

Along with everything else that helped to shape the young Julio, an event that stands out from his childhood is one which he says gave him his "style of aesthetics"; the first time he wore long pants.

In Spain, as elsewhere in Europe, the first wearing of long pants, the pants of a man, is something of a rite of passage. And Julio did not take the event lightly. Inside, he had always felt like a man, a leader; but this was public acknowledgment of that, and he was determined to look the part. "I can remember it as being a trauma," he says, "because I wanted the long pants to be just right." Compounding the challenge was the fact that the boots he was wearing made him feel clumsy— and not without good reason, the boots having been a size too large, bought that way so Julio could wear them for two years. But Julio rose to the occasion, declaring that an "elegant man was starting to be born within me, the type of gentleman that Spain and the rest of the world makes of me." He took from that day a very clear sense of what he calls "the aesthetic function." The idea that it wasn't enough to *be* perfect: one had to *look* perfect as well.

Fittingly, one of the first long walks he took in public, resplendent in his new pants and boots, was with María. He had stayed after her until he'd won her, stolen his first kiss from her, and she remained Julio's girlfriend for over a year. He may not have been a tall young man, but Julio had the guts of Goliath.

Despite his love of excellence, Julio continued to muck his way through his studies. At the time, he was convinced they didn't matter: since he had no stomach for the sight of blood, he had no intention of becoming a doctor like his father. Even though Julio was young, Julio senior was already resigned to that fact. What he intended to be, not surprisingly, was an international soccer star. And as the years passed, he became more and more preoccupied with the sport.

To his credit, Julio did try to partake in other activities at school—never academic ones, of course, but activities which were in the spotlight. Still, it was a credit to his maturity that he was willing to take responsibility in areas outside of sports. Sadly, his track record was abysmal. He joined the choir, but "they threw me out after the first note," Father Anselmo gently taking Julio aside and counseling him, "Stay with football; singing is not for you." Undaunted, the boy tried out for each and every play the school put on. Unfortunately, while he gave very good readings and showed a great deal of enthusiasm, parts were doled out as a reward for good grades instead of acting ability. Julio laments that in every play he ended up doing "a part with only three words and nothing more," a situation which thwarted his "desire to supersede." However, being thwarted in this way only strengthened his resolve to try out for each new production, to show himself and others that very little could keep him down.

In the meantime, he played soccer and he chased girls—always the tallest girls, the prettiest, the ones that other boys admired. Julio didn't want the girls he could have, or even, necessarily, the ones he liked the best. He wanted "the impossible ones," the girls who by all aesthetic criteria were the best. His rate of success admittedly wasn't high, since girls his age still preferred older boys. But, like his repeated failures on the stage, that never discouraged the plucky Julio from trying.

Then, one fateful day, Julio found a third passion, one which, remarkably, would eventually surpass the other two. He isn't certain when it was, but Julio vividly remembers the day that he bought his first record. He usually spent his weekly allowance on Chiclets, sunflower seeds, and soda. But one week he had some money left over and bought a song he'd heard on the radio. Julio had liked the tune, but when he went into the record store he discovered something more: the feel of the disk. "They were quite thick, very thick, and very heavy. Nowadays, you could make five records from one of those." It was as though the voice itself were locked up inside that sleek prison—"dead," as he says, until "you give it life." The texture of the record, and the idea of having the music at your command—the control—delighted the boy, and he began drinking less Coke and buying more records. Not only those by Mina but love songs by everyone from Pedro Vargas to actress Gina Lollobrigida; later, he was particularly fond of Elvis Presley.

"Such a life!" he marvels today, "full of the vulgar

as well as the passionate." In time, he would disavow the "vulgar"—anything which did not originate in his heart—and become a man guided by passion.

Julio's newfound affection for music notwithstanding, soccer remained his greatest passion right through his teenage years. One was private, the other very public; and above all Julio was still a ham, even though he prefers to refer to himself euphemistically as a "protagonist," someone who made good things happen.

As it happened, he was able to indulge himself in soccer to his heart's content. Behind his school, there was a stadium where all the Madrid professionals worked out. If Julio didn't have practice himself, he would rush over to the stadium after classes. Because he belonged to the youth league, he had a pass which allowed him to go inside and, dressed proudly in his goalie's uniform, he would perch attentively in the bleachers and watch them play. He was quite literally mesmerized, "watching practice games between teams in which the ball would pass from heel to heel and from there to the neck without touching the field."

When the players took a break, Julio would study the way his favorites walked and spoke and laughed, and he adopted their mannerisms. He would also run down and ask for their autographs, just to be near them, and had his photograph taken with anyone who would hold still long enough. All of these mementoes went immediately onto the walls of his room.

But Julio really went to town when his friends would accompany him to the stadium. Even the kids who didn't play soccer knew the players, and Julio used that to his advantage. "I would go over and say hello to the professionals," he recalls, "slapping them on the back and calling them by their first name." Though he can't remember ever saying anything that wasn't "nonsense," the players understood what he was doing and played along with him, greeting the boy like an old friend.

As Julio passed from adolescence to young adulthood, he began to lavish less energy on facades and more on genuinely perfecting what was most important to him, his athletic abilities. He did indeed cut a dashing figure on the field, this trim six-footer in his tight T-shirt and shorts. He had, even then, an electric smile, and his preoccupation with exercise had given him lithe, very muscular legs and a torso remarkably like Michelangelo's David.

Yet the more he knuckled down and the more serious he got about his life and efforts, the less people paid attention to him—especially girls. While most athletes tended to have a lot of girlfriends, Julio simply wasn't the archetypal jock. He didn't have a loud, carousing nature, but rather the quiet temperament of a doctor.

In the same way that his father would dispassionately diagnose illnesses, Julio would analyze soccer or his own personality or any other event in his life and then precisely, surgically, cut away the imperfections. He was an *intense* jock. Paradoxically, because all this intensity went to improving himself rather than to purely intellectual pursuits, he was not, in his own word, "brilliant" enough for girls who admired intelligence in men. The young lion who used to entertain them by jumping through hoops had turned to marble, preoccupied with excellence rather than entertainment. And in a world where young people valued the circus more than a museum, Julio ended up being an extremely lonely young man.

CHAPTER THREE

"**A** chronicle of constant dissatisfaction," is how Julio describes his teenage years. He had swung from being an extrovert to being a middlebrow philosopher—a trait he was never to surrender. Today he says that "to talk about women fascinates me. That is the precise word: fascinates. I need them more than life itself; or, to put it another way, they *are* my life." Even so, now as then, Julio says that entering the world of women "is to enter into a territory of extreme sadness—sadness that is my lover of many nights, even though next to me there is a beautiful woman, naked."

Julio's love/hate relationship with women wouldn't truly blossom until the devastating collapse of his marriage years later, from which he might not have recovered without the help of a very compassionate psychiatrist.

But during his high school years, Julio's problems weren't as deep as all that. He had some very good male friends and he had soccer. Only now, it wasn't soccer at the School of the Holy Hearts, but as a goalie on the junior reserve team of the professional and very prestigious Real Madrid Club de Fútbol. Getting on

25

the team was a real coup, and Julio was justifiably
proud. He had dreamed of being on the Madrid team,
and when the experts saw him and then pronounced
him "a valiant goalkeeper . . . pure energy," he was eu-
phoric. However, what excited him nearly as much as
the chance to play on the squad was what his accep-
tance portended: possible appointment to the first string
after a season or two.

Under the watchful eye of trainer Miguel Muñoz,
Julio refined his skills until he was truly a first-class
goalie, so skillful that everyone associated with the
team was convinced he had a promising future in the
sport.

While Julio had always fantasized about becoming a
professional soccer player, the encouragement of the
Real Madrid personnel flamed that desire until it was
quite all-consuming. And as much as he and his parents
had talked about him becoming a lawyer—in time,
shifting to the diplomatic corps—there was no denying
his heart. Julio wanted this, desperately, and he also
wanted his father in particular to want it with him.

Julio senior is a practical man, but not a hard one.
He wasn't about to deny his son, though he did make
one stipulation: he insisted that Julio go for an education, become a lawyer first and then turn his attention
to professional goalkeeping.

Although that was not quite what Julio had wanted
to hear, he saw the sense of it; even if he hadn't, the
young man had too much regard for his father to debate
the point. He would be with the team on weekends and
over vacations, and that would somehow sustain him.

Finishing high school, Julio turned his attention to
finding a university that would suit his purposes. He
had several schools from which to choose: since out-
growing his hyperactive stage, Julio had become, if

not studious, at least a better student, and had managed to pull together some very respectable grades. But after discussing the choices with his parents, and looking with commendable candor into his soul, he decided that the best thing to do was to accept an offer to enroll at Cambridge University in England. As far as his soccer career was concerned, it wasn't the best decision he could have made: shuttling back and forth by air would be expensive as well as exhausting. Ultimately, however, Julio knew that the professional life span of a soccer player is not very long, and that when he hung up his shin guards he would have to do something to earn a living. As a diplomat, it would work to his advantage to know English, and he felt there was no better way to learn it than by going to school in England. Trying to look on the bright side, there was a musical and sexual revolution just getting under way in England, so there were benefits to be had.

In 1960, Julio's lovelife was not much more than it had been since the time he and little María parted company many years before ("I don't know what happened to her," he says with some regret). During that decade, there was only one woman with whom he had any kind of serious relationship, and that briefly. Her name was Carmen, and Julio describes her as "a friend of the family." She was several years older than her lover—which, given the mature way he was carrying himself in those days, was not surprising. And she was one thing more: married. In a way, that was also to be expected for, apart from a clear physical and emotional attraction, Julio was drawn to Carmen *because* she was "forbidden." That made the relationship, in his estimation, "very appealing and beautiful," just like "the Italian movies of that time." To have romance and a logistical challenge both was enormously attractive to him.

Obviously, a relationship with that kind of foundation was foredoomed and, not long after it had begun, the "turbulent love affair" came apart at the seams. It did so, apparently, with some unpleasantness since, unlike young María, Julio says, "I am not interested in knowing" where Carmen is today and adds—a bit vindictively?—"I imagine she must have grandchildren."

Suffice it to say that, grandmother or not, Carmen isn't among the four hundred names in Julio's little red book, a book so dear to him that he "guards it religiously" and keeps a copy "in a corner of my house, like a precious jewel in a Swiss bank," in case the original is ever lost. His astonishing achievements in music aside, Julio has made incredible progress in coming to grips with the opposite sex.

With all the difficulties inherent in moving to another country, Julio adjusted easily to England. In fact, Britain allowed his sartorial sense to flourish: no longer living in soccer clothes, he dressed like a local lord, right down to the bowler, umbrella, and black trenchcoat.

The transition was made particularly easy due to the presence of a small Spanish contingent at the school, of which Julio's close friend and fellow Real Madrid player Enrique Clemente was a member. The two had many memorable times that first year, exploring the country, coaching each other in English, keeping each other soccer trim, and traveling together on their frequent trips home. Julio's grades were good, his social life was active if superficial, and, despite the fears he had harbored, it proved to be one of the most delightful years of his life.

The summer of 1963 was a busy one for the boys. They played soccer together, shared delightful days at the beach, and with their friends Tito Arroyo and Pedro

Luis Iglesias often partied together. Because Julio had the sharp red sportscar, he was the one who usually drove wherever they went; most notably on that fateful day late in the summer when he sped recklessly into Death Curve.

"I do everything big," Julio says with characteristic bluntness. "The bad? Worse than anybody else. Ten times as wrong. *Unsurpassably* wrong, for I do not have a middle ground. But when I'm good," he goes on without false modesty, "I'm better than anybody."

Both of these qualities would come into play during the next two years, years of physical pain and self-reproach. There wasn't a day that passed without Julio replaying in his mind that awful moment when he realized that he was going to lose control, that there was no way he could stop them from rocketing over the incline.

As he lay in the car, staring through the shattered windshield, he was enveloped by what he describes as a sense of the "sepulchral." The past few moments were a blur, and the present was dreamlike; his only ties to reality were an insistent pain in his chest and heat which was welling through his entire body. He didn't turn to look at his companions; he needed a few moments more to collect himself before turning to face the results of his folly.

"Damn!"

The oath was one of the sweetest things Julio had ever heard. He wasn't sure who had called out, but was grateful that someone else, at least, had survived. His relief positively soared as, still lying there, he heard the broken metal of the door creak and he heard, one by one, his friends struggling from the car. He finally glanced over and saw that while their clothes were shredded and the young men were cut, bruised, and dirty, at least they were alive. Julio thanked God and began to wonder about his second gravest concern: not what injuries he might have sustained, but how he would possibly explain what had happened to his father.

Lying there, he heard one of his friends ask another, "How are you?"

Someone answered, "I'm all right, I guess—except for my back."

The third boy groaned as he came around the car.

"And you?" asked the first.

"I'll live, though I feel like my kidneys have been pulverized."

"Be thankful," advised the first. "It's a miracle any of us is even *alive!*"

There was a subdued exchange—Julio wondered if they were talking about each other or about him—after which the three of them trudged to his side. The door had popped open upon impact, and Enrique knelt while the others looked on, dour expressions on their smudged faces.

"Julio," his friend asked softly, "can you move?"

Julio wasn't sure he wanted to find out. "I don't know," he replied. "My chest hurts and so does my stomach."

"Do you want to try and get up?"

"I don't think that's a good idea," Tito put in. "If he's hurt, you may only aggravate the injury. Maybe I should go back to town and get a doctor."

Cautious Tito, Julio thought. Of course he realized that he should have listened to Tito before, on the curve; perhaps he should listen to him now as well. But the notion of summoning a doctor sent shock waves through Julio, for to do so meant to acknowledge that he might well be hurt, that he might have sustained more than a few bumps or broken bones. The thought was not only unacceptable to Julio, it was unthinkable. *I can get up*, he told himself. And even if his muscles didn't *want* to work, he would make them do so just the same.

"I—I think I'm all right," he told Enrique, then painfully raised his arms from the seat. The boys jumped to help him, raising him gently, slowly, hands under his neck, behind his head, around his shoulders, as though they were lifting a newborn from its mother. It's an appropriate metaphor, for some time later Julio would declare, "I was born a second time after my accident on that dusty road." Which is not to say that Julio was changed: he wasn't. Julio had not been reborn in the same way that recovery from a debilitating ailment changes most people, putting the world into perspective and teaching them to delight in life's little pleasures. Quite the contrary. After going through hell over the next two years, Julio Iglesias would emerge with his belief reinforced that he only prospers when faced with an extraordinary challenge.

In fact, after two years of suffering, Julio did not return to the mainstream of life filled with a sense of pride or triumph, but with the very real problem of what to do for an encore.

CHAPTER FOUR

With the help of his friends, Julio stood up.

Apart from the pain of the bruises, and the odd, tingling warmth which now filled him from head to foot, he didn't feel as though he'd sustained a serious injury. Outwardly, he was abraded far less than his companions; unlike them, his clothes weren't even torn. But Julio wasn't exactly relieved, for he still had to face his father.

Julio walked a few paces up the incline, through the cloud of smoke that was pouring from the engine. Though each step caused a smarting pain along his lower back and sides, he knew he could make it back to town. With a last, skeptical glance from Tito, the foursome set off, eyes cast to the ground, the silence punctuated only when one or the other of the boys muttered something about how amazing it was they were all in one piece.

As they walked, Julio became aware of what he describes as "a terrible fear," something nameless and vague but palpable just the same. He attributed it to the shock of the accident, but years later, in his metaphysical way, he would come to regard it as an omen, a psychic recognition of the fact that, despite appearances, all was not well with Julio Iglesias.

The first place they reached was a bar just outside of town. They went inside, drawing alarmed stares from the few people inside. Julio asked to use the telephone and, calling his father's clinic, was relieved to hear that he had gone home hours before. Rather than call home and wake his parents, Julio related what had happened and asked if someone would drive over and pick them up.

Brought to the clinic, the boys were cleaned up and given a quick examination. The doctors were even more astonished than the' boys that no one had been badly hurt. One of the men on the night shift eventually drove them home.

It was four A.M. when Julio walked in the front door. Unable to move with his usual grace, he raised such a clamor that his parents woke up; he says that they hurried out and, after looking at him once, didn't look at him again. There was a look of shock on their faces, and Julio recalls that as they listened to his story, "My father was frightened, but not as much as my mother." Rosario's expression shaded from disbelief to relief, and when he was finished, he remembers her saying simply, softly, "Son, the main thing is that you're alive."

But if it was a joy his father shared, he didn't show it. As Julio had expected, the elder Iglesias was "furious" and, standing there in his robe, snapped, "Julio, you're *very* inconsiderate."

"I know . . . I'm sorry," Julio replied sheepishly.

There was a heavy silence as Julio's father stared harshly at the young man. Julio's gaze fell. Then, realizing that his son had been through an ordeal, the elder man's features softened slightly. After a momen he said more charitably, "Promise me that you'll be more careful in the future."

Julio nodded, forcing a weak smile, and without returning the smile, his father went back to bed. Standing there alone, Julio marveled at how he'd gotten off as easily as he did, both physically and emotionally. He was repentant, of course, but more than that he was grateful. The next day he would apologize to his friends, smooth it all out, and everything would be fine.

Looking down at his shoes, which were scuffed and gashed, he sighed with relief, smiled, and shuffled off to bed.

Julio returned to school early in October, and resumed his weekend activities on the soccer field. "I ran, jumped, walked, threw the ball," he says, "all of this with complete normalcy." Then, within a few days of getting back into his regular routine, he says simply, "I began to feel a pain."

The pain started in his back. "It felt like a needle penetrating my skin. No, more than that: I felt like it was going right through the bone itself." At first, Julio's pains were irregular. He would have them for a few minutes one day, then not the next; sometimes they would hit him when he was active, other times when he was sitting.

"Now, I was a very physical and strong person," he says, "but those pains were unbearable, the worst I'd ever experienced in my life." And the unbearable quickly got worse. The pains no longer went away after a few minutes, but started lasting much longer. Then they came every day, sometimes more than once. Finally, they were no longer localized in his back, but could crop up along his limbs or in his chest. The pains in his chest were the worst of all, since when they struck it was sheer agony to breathe. And they started coming at night as well as in the day, causing him to lose countless hours of sleep.

For a while, Julio kept the pain to himself, not even telling his parents. It wasn't machismo on his part, but an unwillingness to accept the fact that the pains might be there to stay. If he told his parents, they would make him go to the doctor; if he did that, the doctor might find something wrong and, again, Julio didn't want to know that there was something wrong with him. That he could be reduced to something less than other people.

But as stubborn as he could be, there was a point at which even Julio had to capitulate. The pains grew so severe that they were "scary," and when his suffering manifested itself as dark bags under his eyes and uncharacteristic irritability, Julio spoke to his parents. His father arranged an appointment with a local specialist, and Julio was relieved when he finally went to be examined. Pride be damned, there would be an end to the pain. But the examination turned up nothing, leaving Julio right back where he started.

"I went to other doctors, specialists, clinics, friends of my father," he says. "There were studies, X rays, but everybody always said the same thing. 'Doctor Iglesias, there is nothing wrong with your son. Or at least nothing we can find.'" A few of the doctors thought that Julio's problem might stem from nerves, so in addition to painkillers they prescribed relaxants.

"I took as many pills as I could," confesses Julio, indicating just how severe the pain was. Until then, he had been so opposed to introducing chemicals into his system that he'd been reluctant to take even an aspirin. Now, he says, he gulped down "pills, tablets, anything to kill that terrible pain."

While the medication was able to dull the pain, it never offered complete relief; eventually, even the pills stopped working. "One afternoon I sneezed," he says, wincing at the memory, "and the pain was so strong that it broke me. It was a ferocious *pull*, and I lost consciousness." Afterward, he continues, "it became normal that I would lose consciousness when the pain struck."

And the pain struck more constantly than before. "I noticed that my father was very worried now," he says, "and he stayed with me constantly." Julio did not return to school, though he doggedly stayed with his soccer practice—Tuesday, Wednesday, and Friday in nearby Deportiva, and Thursdays at the stadium. All the while he hoped that keeping his spirits up would help fight the pain if it were psychological in nature—and praying that on the field, at least, while he was doing what he loved most, the pain "would not attack me like a traitor" and leave him unable to play.

In the meantime, Julio and his father traveled to see every osteopath and neurologist they could dig up. But, says the singer, "the doctors continued to say the same thing. With hat-lights on and eyeglasses perched on their forehead, they would say, 'Nothing. Your son has nothing at all.'"

November arrived, and with it came yet another setback. In addition to the spasms, Julio started to notice that whenever he ran during soccer practice his legs would feel wobbly. His trainer saw at once that Julio wasn't getting to the ball as quickly as before and, taking Julio aside, quietly suggested that maybe he was hurting because he wasn't getting *enough* exercise.

"Walk!" he encouraged the boy. "That's what you have to do, man. That's why your teammates run better than you do, because they never had a car. Don't fix the old car, don't get a new car, don't get a ride here. Just walk!"

Julio tried, but good intentions weren't enough. By December, his legs were weaker still, and finally, while he was standing on a curb, waiting to cross a street near his home, his legs gave out entirely. Julio managed to get back up and struggle home, where he all but fell into his father's arms.

"What am I going to do?" the boy asked, not with self-pity but from sheer frustration. His father looked at him and, says Julio, "with desperation in his eyes, said, 'Son, we have seen nearly fifty doctors, and there doesn't seem to be a logical, scientific explanation for whatever is wrong with you.'" He promised to continue talking to his colleagues, and asked his son to try and be patient. Julio promised he would try and, meanwhile, halfheartedly suggested that perhaps if he started driving again, put less strain on his legs, they might improve. His father agreed—most likely to humor Julio more than anything else—but while the young man didn't collapse again, his reflexes continued to deteriorate.

"I became clumsy, heavy," he says. "At times, I looked like dead weight." His father, he says, would come along and "observe me in silence," after which they'd return home and Dr. Iglesias would make calls to colleagues around the country. Even when he had to work at the clinic, half his time would be spent on the telephone, looking for anyone who might have some answers. And each time he found someone they would go, Julio describing it as "a cavalry of doctors with more X rays, more sitting in waiting rooms, more consultations."

Christmas 1963 was especially difficult for the family, because everyone tried to be festive, though no one really felt like it. "It was truly horrible," Julio says with a shudder. "I had wanted to enjoy the day of the Wise

Men, for it to be a pleasant memory for my family, if not for me. But I was being destroyed, and the exception, now, was not to have the pain." On top of that, his equilibrium and coordination continued to go "downhill. I was losing strength in all my muscles and was very scared, even though I tried to be very strong and didn't tell anybody."

But his parents and Carlos knew, of course, even though they didn't let on. They could see it in his movements, in his face. And having to keep up the facade for Julio's sake only made the season that much more difficult to get through.

Then, on January 1, his iron will finally broke down and Julio let the pain express itself. Not that it was a matter of choice: "I just couldn't bear it," he admits. The pain was so bad along his back and limbs that he virtually became a cripple, literally unable to do anything more than "scream, cry, and crawl."

Dr. Iglesias quickly rallied a group of his colleagues to discuss a plan of action. Having spent over two months listening to his peers and conducting endless research on his own, he had come to the conclusion that Julio's problem was clearly not with his bones, nor his nerves, nor his mind, but was probably due to a clot or growth of some kind that was causing his vertebrae to compress, something that the examinations would not necessarily have revealed.

The elder Iglesias aired his theory, one which the others admitted they had also begun to consider. Unfortunately, there was no more time to reflect or commiserate. Dr. Franco Manera, an internist, made the suggestion that they get Julio to the clinic at once and "see what the Tiodoro says," a process that would let them see into the young man's spine.

Dr. Iglesias agreed, though even as they made

ready to move Julio he had grave reservations. If the diagnosis were correct, there was a good possibility that the clot or growth might be inoperable due to its proximity to the spinal cord. If he were wrong, not only were they back at square one with nowhere to turn, but "el Tiodoro" itself could kill his boy.

Still, there was nothing else to try, and as 1964 dawned the now-gaunt twenty-year-old Julio Iglesias found himself being helped into the car for an experience which, twenty years later, he cannot discuss without prefacing his remarks with a quiet, still agonized, "God almighty."

CHAPTER FIVE

"Nowadays, I believe that there are more modern methods to investigate one's back. And if it isn't so, I *wish* it, with all the strength of my soul. I wish it because I don't want anybody to have to go through what I went through that January."

Having been given a room and dressed in a hospital gown, Julio, nearly paralyzed, was thereafter taken to Block Zero and placed, seated upright, on the operating table.

Before that day, Julio says that he always regarded himself as a man of some fortitude and courage. However, what he discovered as he was carried into the sterile, white room was that he was quite capable of feeling "the terror of a child." Though he internalized it, his terror was absolute, physical as well as spiritual. Physically, he couldn't help but fear the needle he saw awaiting him near the operating table, "the very long, very big, very thick needle" which they'd be pushing down his neck. He had overheard that, for some reason or another, he would not be given an anesthetic, and it was a prospect he couldn't even begin to imagine.

Spiritually, he feared dying, of "not being anything" if something went wrong. Even the hope that he would finally learn what was at the root of his suffering did little to ease Julio's anxiety.

Indeed, the only consolation—and it should not be underestimated—was that his father would be present the entire time. Dr. Iglesias had been on hand when Julio was born, making difficult decisions about the baby's life and death. Though this was not his field, Dr. Iglesias had insisted on being there for his son's "rebirth" as well. Julio derived a great deal of comfort from knowing that if anything could make the procedure less difficult, his father would see that it was done.

Once Julio was settled on top of the table, one of the doctors came over and patiently explained what they were about to do.

"We are going to inject a red dye, which will travel along your vertebral column and through the spinal cord. Once inside, the liquid will stain the tissues, allowing us to see them on an X ray. Then we will know if there is anything there." Clasping Julio on the shoulder, he went on, "But we cannot put you to sleep, for you must hold yourself perfectly still." Julio was told that if he moved, the needle could permanently injure or even kill him.

As the young man tried to digest all of this, the doctor indicated four sets of straps on the table. These, he explained, would be used to tie Julio at the wrists and ankles to make certain he didn't jerk or squirm at any time. His paralysis, though severe, was not absolute, and so these precautions had to be taken.

With an encouraging nod from his father, a very pale Julio offered the attendants his hands and feet. He did so mechanically, as though watching it happen to somebody else. Concurrently, some small, masochistic corner of his mind became active, torturing him with visions of rabbits being skewered, bulls being stabbed, and sheep being stabbed. Julio didn't know whether his subconscious was trying to prepare him for the worst, or whether it was telling him that things *could* be worse. All he wanted to do was drive the images from his mind, which he did by telling himself "thousands and thousands of times that this was not to kill me, but to give me life."

Once he had been secured "like a person that is going to be electrocuted," Julio was told to bow his head forward and keep it there. The needle was to be inserted from above, straight down. His insides churning, his heart drumming, Julio looked down at the metal tabletop. Suddenly aware of how cold it was on his bare legs, he tried to concentrate on that, trying not to hear the doctors "murmuring all around me," or look at their feet poking from beneath their long gowns as they moved the equipment into position.

"We'.e going to start, Julio."

The youth didn't know whose voice it was, and didn't really care. He shut his eyes, trying to obliterate the mental picture of that needle, that "long sewing needle," whose fine point was just now pressed against the nape of his neck. Then the procedure was begun.

The initial prick caused Julio's knees to tighten reflexively, and he immediately forced them to calm. He told himself that this was another María, another Real Madrid, another impossible situation which he must somehow dominate.

Slowly, the needle moved into his neck, "penetrating through my skin, layer after layer after layer. I swear," Julio says today, "it was terrible . . . a very slow agony in which you know everything that's being done to you." He adds, "That while the red liquid could not be *heard* going in, he could *feel* it."

Julio doesn't remember how many minutes he sat there, feeling the cool dye moving slowly under his skin, but he remembers the moment it ended. As soon as the needle was withdrawn, the slow-motion pace of the doctors accelerated as he was quickly untied and "put on a platform for more X rays, on my feet like Spartacus crucified."

After he was X-rayed, Julio was returned to his room. Drained by his agonies and dizzy from painkillers, he wasn't sure how much later they informed him that they had found the problem: a small, well-hidden tumor which was compressing his spine and causing the bones to pinch the nerves of his back and limbs. "I was told they had to operate, and that it had to be done quickly," he says. "If not, the compression would have left me like a broken doll or killed me altogether."

At the time, the doctors were divided as to just what had caused the tumor to grow, though the most likely reason seemed to be a bodily trauma caused by the car crash. Regardless, the debate was put on the back burner while Julio was prepared for surgery.

He shakes his head. "Once again I was brought to the operating theater, this time stretched out on my stomach. On the way I saw my father, his eyes anguished, telling me everything without saying anything. I also saw my mother. She was crying but also said nothing."

The nurses who were with Julio were the same nurses who worked with his father day after day. Julio knew them and they knew him, and their presence was a comfort to him. His arms were placed on extensions, perpendicular to his body, so the doctors would have complete access to his lower back. An IV was placed in his right arm, tubes were run into his nose, and when everything was ready someone came over to give him an injection.

"You're going to fall asleep," one of the nurses said as he was given the anesthesia, "but don't worry. When you wake up, everything is going to be fine. You'll be playing soccer again soon, champion!"

Julio smiled weakly, the woman's voice being the next-to-last thing he remembers before passing out. The last thing he remembers? Not that he was a sheep, a bull, or a rabbit, but that this time he was a *pig* being readied for portioning. . . .

When the world came back into focus, Julio found himself staring at the same white wall he'd been looking at when he'd gone to sleep.

He said, "What's this? Hasn't anything happened yet?" At least, those were the words he'd formed in his mind. What came out, what he'd heard himself mumble, was another matter.

A moment later, one of the nurses came over. "Be calm," she said, smiling. "They have already operated."

"How—how long?" Julio asked, taking pains to say the words clearly.

One of the doctors walked over. "It took eight hours," he said. He was not smiling, but that didn't bother Julio. The nurse's smile had been enough for him. "Exactly eight hours."

Confused, Julio shut his eyes, dimly aware of extreme coldness up and down his back and inside his body. His old pain, his "friend," was gone, but that was not all: as he dozed off, he realized that except for the ice inside of him he felt no sensations at all, from his waist to the heels of both feet.

The next thing Julio knew he was back in his room,

with his family gathered around him. More alert than before, he immediately recalled his half-formed fears from the operating room and tried to move his legs. He found, to his horror, that it had been no nightmare. He was completely paralyzed below the waist.

He tried to speak, but there was a tube in his mouth and the words came out garbled. His father told him to lie still, pointing out that he mustn't disturb the bandages around his body, not to mention the tubes that were still in his nose and the IV in his arm. Carrying his chair closer to the bed, the elder Iglesias took his son's hand in his own.

"Whatever it is that's wrong with you, give it time," he softly urged, feeling none of the confidence he was trying to project. "We have removed a cyst from your spinal column, the growth that has been responsible for everything. The bone is clean and intact, and you're going to be fine." He forced a smile and patted the young man's limp hand. "You have suffered a lot, son, but everything is finished. Trust me, you're going to bounce right back."

Julio stared into his father's eyes, wanting to believe him if for no other reason than it would be unthinkable to be restricted to a bed or a wheelchair, not to be able to run, to walk, to lead the vital life he'd enjoyed just a few months before. But his father's eyes were dull and sad, reflecting anything but the hope of which he'd just spoken.

Julio looked from his brother to his mother. Carlos was smiling broadly, as usual; his mother was smiling less so, showing her motherly concern. And when he looked back at his father, Julio saw that Dr. Iglesias was not smiling at all. His inclination was to try and interpret their expressions, but he realized that that would be fruitless: these people were family. They hurt for him, he could see it in their faces. And they were obviously exhausted, just as muddled as he was at that moment.

Instead of looking outward, Julio shut his eyes and looked inward. *It will pass*, he told himself. *The paralysis will pass*. His body would heal itself or, as he'd vowed back on the road that dark September night, he would somehow *make* it heal. He would not be beaten down.

But, as he was later to learn, his parents were concerned about more than just the paralysis. At that moment, a biopsy was being performed on the tumor they'd removed from Julio. And while there was every reason to believe that the growth had been caused by the accident, there was also the very real possibility that it was malignant. And for all his son's grit and bravado, Dr. Iglesias did not believe that even the tenacious Julio could pull the rug out from under cancer.

CHAPTER SIX

Despite Julio's testimony, there is some doubt as to whether it was the accident which caused all of his problems. The shock to his nervous system could very well have caused a neuroma, a tumor of the nerve tissue—but Julio does not say that the growth was anything of the sort. The accident could also have exacerbated an existing ailment, though a preexisting condition would eventually have surfaced in any event.

Regardless, over twenty years ago, considerably less was known about these problems or their origins than is known today, and they were treated in something of a scattershot method.

Julio was lying in his bed the day after the operation, his mother seated beside him, where she had spent the night. Sedated, Julio looked up groggily when José Luis, the family chauffeur and a dead ringer for Robert Duvall, burst into his room.

"Benign, *señor*. Benign!"

Rosario, who had spent the night by her son's side, stared at the chauffeur. "Benign?" she asked. José nod-

ded, beaming, and the woman sighed deeply. Julio's
father walked in moments later.

"Did you tell them, José?"

"Yes, señor."

"You see?" He smiled at Julio. "There is nothing to
worry about."

"I—I don't understand. What is this 'benign'?"

Dr. Iglesias shook his head. "It's the name of the
surgeon who removed your tumor." Julio looked on
with a puzzled expression, and the elder Iglesias came
closer. "You should have studied harder at school! It
means that the tumor is not malignant. It means you do
not have cancer."

Having been unaware that anyone thought he might
have cancer, Julio was alarmed and at the same time
consoled. But his relief was short-lived. The next day,
one of the doctors met with Julio's father to suggest that
they give the young man radiation treatment all the
same. Though the tumor itself wasn't cancerous, the
doctors could not be sure there weren't other, smaller
growths that had not shown up on the X rays, tumors
growing in places where the surgeons had been unable
to look.

The recommendation did not sit well with Dr.
Iglesias, who knew that radiation, if abused, could be as
destructive as cancer. But he also knew that if there
were invisible and inoperable tumors, and they weren't
destroyed now, they might be too large to irradiate in
the future. Once again, Julio's father was faced with a
Catch-22 which beleaguered the doctor in him and
tormented the parent. Finally deciding that it was
better to risk the radiation than chance the tumors, he
reluctantly gave his okay for cobalt treatments.

Once again Dr. Iglesias concealed the truth from
his son, telling Julio that the radiation was being used

to try and activate his legs. Each day for two weeks, Julio was brought into another white room where, for three to four minutes, he was placed "under a terrible apparatus and subjected to an invisible fire." And, quite simply, the doctors kept this up until Julio began to have serious negative reactions to the treatment. "I started to lose white corpuscles, and it was like I had water in my veins. I had no strength, and I had no appetite. Sometimes my lungs were so tired they didn't even want to breathe. I felt like I was dying . . . slowly."

When it became apparent that Julio was too frail to continue, the treatments were halted. Still being fed intravenously, he was down to ninety-nine pounds and describes himself as "only bones." His arms weren't paralyzed, but he could barely move them all the same. No one was certain what the radiation had accomplished, the prevailing attitude being one of all-is-said-and-done. Julio's fate was no longer in the doctors' hands, but in the lap of the gods.

As his strength returned, Julio regained the use of his arms, but not his legs. "I would lie there," he says, "and I would tell my head and my feet and my legs, 'Move, dammit, move.' But though my head said yes, the rest of my body said no."

The days dragged on and Julio's spirits plummeted. He didn't speak, and refused to take solid foods; fearing the consequences of Julio's depression, his father decided to bring him back home. Medically, he didn't think the change of scenery would do him a bit of good. But Julio was a creature governed by psychology, and Dr. Iglesias hoped that in that sense the move might prove significant.

After making a few changes in the room—brighter lights and a movable hospital bed were brought in, along with a medicine cabinet for convenience—Dr. Iglesias took his son home. There were no banners, no fanfare, no welcome-home gifts or boxes of candy. Julio had been discharged to take a vacation. This was still his home, and his father wanted him to be comfortable there, but there was also work to be done. Dr. Iglesias didn't know if his son would ever walk again, but he meant to create the proper psychological environment for him to try.

The only real misstep Dr. Iglesias made during his son's convalescence occurred the day after he brought his son home. That was when he brought a wheelchair home from the clinic. He'd briefly considered using the chair as a form of negative psychology, telling Julio what he'd be in for if he didn't get back on his feet. But he discarded that as cruel and a burden his son didn't need. Instead, he brought the wheelchair in and told Julio that it was there simply as a means of giving him a bit of freedom. "You're not going to be in it for very long," he concluded, "but in the meantime it will make life just a little more convenient."

Though his father's motive was sincere, Julio would not hear of it. He gazed at the great wheels, "that cold metal . . . and in that wheelchair I did not see my life, but my death." Julio didn't say anything, but after a few seconds his eyes locked on those of his father, holding them firmly, defiantly. Dr. Iglesias may not have meant to "challenge" Julio in so many words, but that was how his son took it. They continued to stare at each other for a long minute, after which, he says, his father "simply lowered his head and left, taking the wheelchair with him. It was never mentioned again."

The impact of that image, his father beside the chair, is one Julio describes as the most "unforgettable" in his life. It was love and pain and futility in one desolate moment, a vision so powerful that Julio says, "Even though it has been twenty years, I still feel a trauma every time I see a wheelchair. Each time I see one I have to stop what I'm doing and recover."

The problem with the impressionable-as-ever Julio was that his resolve refused to circulate below the waist. As much as he wanted to walk, his limbs refused to respond. He exercised his arms and torso, hoping to stimulate his legs. He tried his own negative psychology, telling himself that he'd die if he didn't walk, that he'd simply rot away. His parents helped by suppressing the compassion they felt and staying away from Julio unless he asked for their help.

Nothing worked.

Days became weeks, and each day, he says, "I would throw off the covers and look at my feet—look at them *aging*—and order my legs to move. I would even say it, 'Yes, *move*—a tiny bit, just for a second.'" But they didn't budge. "I did that for eighteen hours a day, struggling, and each day I lay there was like a year . . . sweating, holding on, screaming without raising my voice. *Begging*. Asking my legs to do something, and almost going crazy when they didn't." Whenever he became particularly frustrated, he would call in his father, ask him to touch his legs to see if he could feel a muscle move or a tendon twitch. It was always difficult for Dr. Iglesias to say that he had not, but he would never fail to add that one day the answer would be different, that something *would* move.

Remarkably, Julio never gave up, refusing to panic even when he realized that on top of paralysis he had no sexual urges whatsoever. He told himself that his legs were his girlfriends, and that that was handful enough for now.

After a few weeks, he began trying new tacks.

Sometimes, after his parents had gone to bed, he would struggle from bed and pull himself through the house, on the floor like a slug, hoping that if part of the machine moved, all of it might kick in. Whether he was being masochistic or brave is difficult to say, for at the same time he stopped using his soccer career for motivation. Instead, he told himself that if he wasn't going to drag himself into the street, that if he didn't walk to the door, he would not be going outside. No wheelchair, no one carrying him: he would get out under his own steam or not at all.

And then, one day, fired by that singular combination of self-flagellation and sheer force of will, Julio Iglesias did at last move a toe.

When he saw it wiggle, and knew that it was *he* who had caused the toe to move, Julio screamed. He cried out that a miracle had happened, and his parents and brother came rushing in. He said nothing but, rather, with a supreme effort, repeated the miracle for them. His family watched it struggle to and fro, and when Julio dropped back exhausted, the four of them fell into one big embrace, crying on each other, praising Julio, and thanking God—in that order.

His voice is triumphant, even today, when Julio recalls that moment. "I finally did it. After all those days of sending urgent messages and telegrams from head to leg I *did* it." He laughs. "It was only the big toe on my left foot, but to me it was like the raising of Lazarus."

CHAPTER SEVEN

With the wisdom of hindsight, Julio says, "I had never thought about my health before. I had always had it; I was as strong as a bull. I didn't know what it was like to feel well until I no longer *was* well."

That achievement of moving his toe, after a month of prostration, cannot be underestimated. Yet as far as the hyperdemanding young man was concerned, no sooner had it been accomplished than it was no longer significant. It was just a toe—not a foot, not a leg, and certainly not enough to stand on. He added two hours a day to his regimen, sleeping just four hours a night, and set himself the impossible task of moving something new each and every day. Incredibly, he practically reached his goal.

Still lying flat on his back, Julio decided that the first order of business was to build his strength so that he could at least sit up without having to raise the back of the bed. He ate red meat "like a cannibal . . . meat, meat, always meat," and four days after he had moved his toe, he was able to struggle into a sitting position. In the days that followed, he regained the movement of more toes, then his feet; and finally, after nearly two months of being bedridden, an uplifted Julio Iglesias sent an invitation to his legs to move, and one of them responded by bending ever so slightly.

And once again, that was not enough. No sooner had he gotten both legs to twitch than he asked his father and brother to take him under the arms and walk him around the room. With great patience and even greater joy, they stood beside him for the ninety minutes it took Julio to sit, swing his legs over the bed, plant his feet on the floor, stand erect, and take his first glorious step. The effort to achieve that thoroughly exhausted Julio, and he immediately collapsed in their arms. There was no weeping this time but laughter, as joy finally replaced hope in the Iglesias household.

Waking at eight o'clock each day, after four hours of sleep, Julio began his self-originated rehabilitation with fresh efforts to walk. He was determined to rack up at least one additional step every time he was helped from bed, and he did it. He also asked for mirrors to be hung in his room and in the hall. In the small hours of the night, from ten o'clock to three or four A.M., when he engaged in his ritual of crawling about, he would pause by the mirros and look at himself. He would burn the image of that still-helpless young man in his mind and, rededicated to his goal, quickly move on, telling himself that he was not a cripple but a mountain lion. That fantasy, that image of sinew and confidence, helped Julio to slink rather than lurch, to move his hips, thighs, and feet in tandem as he crept along.

During this period of recuperation, Julio never considered what might happen if at some point the progress stopped. It was never really clear whether there had been any damage to his spinal cord, a nick or scratch which might stop his mobility dead at a certain level. But while Julio refused to think about it, his subconscious brought it up over and over. Many times he would wake up from his brief sleep panting and sweating, worrying that he might make no further progress or, worse, lose ground. He became especially paranoid about his equilibrium, not only the act of movement but the quality of movement. If the floor seemed to weave, he'd pause and make it stop. If he were walking forward, he would suddenly ask for help shuffling sideways, to make sure that he could make the adjustment without faltering. There mustn't be a single weak link in the chain of his rehabilitation. He cursed his mind for troubling him with additional burdens, but at the same time they helped to keep up his concentration.

Though Julio still couldn't walk on his own, he decided that it was time to give himself a taste of something he desperately wanted. Thus, he asked his parents to take him outside and, standing by the street, Julio smiled as he savored the bright light, felt the spring sun on his face as he watched the cars pass. Once having sampled it, he told himself that if he wanted more of the same, he'd have to earn it. And, though it was the equivalent of running a daily marathon, each day Julio tried to do just that.

When he was showing sufficient strength and coordination, Julio was put on a program of daily workouts in the pool at a local rehabilitition center. He would go right after breakfast, and the experience provided both a physical and a psychological boost. As he went through his four-hour routine, he would study the other people at the pool, those who were totally or partly but in any case *permanently* paralyzed. He saw the bitterness in their expressions as they sat with their legs dangling in the water, and for the first time he was able to step outside himself, to see how truly lucky he was. Not only was he recovering, but he hadn't experienced even a hint of self-pity. That, he knew, had given him a very critical edge.

After his daily swim, Julio would be driven to Casa de Campo in Madrid, where he would always order a huge steak sandwich in the restaurant there. The thought of eating a sandwich that size today gives Julio pause, but back then he would eat it whether he was hungry or not. Then he would enter the park and walk about. Julio no longer required anyone to hold him, but walked with a pair of metal crutches, the kind which reach to the elbow.

Since his father was back working on a regular schedule, and his mother was busy keeping house, they could not go with him on these trips as often as they would have liked. Thus, Julio was usually accompanied by the devoted José Luis and by Rock, a German shepherd. A friend had given the dog to Julio to help keep his spirits up, and in no time flat Rock had become "like a very small brother of mine, very much a family member." Sometimes Carlos would go with them and the two of them would race. Carlos would spot him several kilometers and, boasts Julio, "I always won." It was only symbolic, of course, but it meant a great deal to the young man.

Each day in the park, Julio made a little bit more progress. He would walk a little faster, rely slightly less on the crutches, and increase his distance as well. Rosario says she would always know how far Julio had gone by how long Rock continued to pant when they returned. At home, Julio continued his rehabilitation, metal hand rails having been installed around the house so that he could walk rather than crawl. The first day they went to the park, Julio only managed to walk some twenty meters; before the summer was out he was covering "twenty kilometers daily, eight hours of walking without stopping." Once he had reached that level, José Luis no longer bothered to walk behind him. There was now very little danger of Julio falling, and, besides, the chauffeur had grown cross due to severe weight loss from all the exercise.

Julio cherishes those months he spent in the park. When he was tired, he would pause and lean on a tree and carve his name in the bark; soon, there wasn't a trunk along the route which didn't bear his mark. He came to know every inch of the park, "stone by stone, corner to corner," and is convinced that, even today, he could walk it blindfolded. He also came to love the park regulars: the groundskeepers, the police officers, the people who came there to sit or read or eat a bag lunch. They always asked Julio how he was doing, and their genuine affection was one more thing that kept Julio going.

He also came to know the lovers, and they were the ones who delighted him the most. He didn't know them by face, or by any other part of their anatomy, since the cast of players was always changing. But he knew them by their universal manner, the sounds and expressions which came from behind the bushes, the satisfied grins as they emerged, the sense of being the only ones in the world as they walked away, hand in hand. Watching them reawakened the dormant lover in Julio, and while he was not yet ready to jump back into circulation, he was glad to see that that part of him had not died.

Through it all, that long year of relearning to walk, what uplifted Julio the most, however, was not the people or even his progress, but the fact that not once did he experience his old "friend," the pain. Nor was

there anything to indicate that the doctors' worst fears
would be realized, that there were other tumors in
Julio's back. After beginning 1964 in the depths of pain
and fear, Julio ended the year with a genuine feeling of
pride and thanksgiving.

By the following spring, Julio was no longer measuring his progress by steps and kilometers. He moved
through the park like a sprinter, smiling broadly as
Rock ran round him like a faithful little satellite. The
only time that Julio felt at all self-conscious was during
the summer, when the family took its traditional trip to
Peniscola. He would be appearing as a semi-invalid
before those people who used to cheer him on as he
rode his bicycle, and that was a difficult pill to swallow.
   "I don't know how I'm going to do it this time," he
confessed to José Luis before they left. "To be seen in
Peniscola with these crutches." But he compensated by
outperforming everyone in the water, swimming five or
six kilometers each morning without resting—often so
far out that the lifeguard would have to ignore the other
bathers just to keep an eye on Julio.
   He not only survived the summer but, come the
fall, he also gave up his crutches for a cane. It was clear
now that it would only be a matter of time before he
regained the full use of his legs. And no sooner had that
become apparent than Julio turned his thoughts from
walking to women.
   Around seven P.M. each day, after his long consti-
tutional through the park, Julio would have José Luis
take him to a café on the Marqués de Urquijo. Because
the road gave access to the university, it was always full
of young women, and Julio reveled in them. "After
having been in my room for such a long time," he sums

it all up, "it was a pleasure just to sit and look at those
pretty girls and their legs."

Julio would order a Coke or orange drink, once in
a while a beer, and then nurse it for an hour or two. He
usually gave his cane to José Luis, who would leave and
sit with it in the car; only when Julio needed to feel
more in control did he keep it with him, under the
table, since he still couldn't walk without it. And there
he would sit, looking out at the girls and delighting
when they looked back at him.

"I felt like a prince," he reveals, "well-dressed and
flirting with the girls." He especially enjoyed the mys-
tique that grew up around him. The people who saw
him day after day wanted to know who this charming
young man was, sitting very quietly, always alone, and
never talking about who he was or why he came to the
café day after day. But Julio kept them in the dark, not
only because he enjoyed being an object of fascination
but also because he didn't want anyone's pity or compassion. What he wanted was to begin his life again.
And each day, after spending some time taking in the
crowd, Julio would select a favorite girl among them,
then try to get her to come to his table. Whether he
succeeded or failed, after that girl left Julio himself
would leave, always alone. He wanted each day to be "a
bit like a novel, a love story like the ones you can buy
in paperback." A tale with a beginning, a middle, and a
bittersweet ending. That final loneliness was an important part of the game: he never wanted to leave without
a reason to pull himself together and return the following day.

Ironically, Julio probably could have had many
women, since he looked better now than ever before.
Bronzed from his long days in the sun, he had also
developed extremely broad shoulders thanks to the

crutches and his all-meat diet. He acknowledges that "from the belly button up" he actually looked quite impressive—but still not ready to return wholeheartedly to the world of physical love.

Besides, during the year and a half he'd spent recovering, Julio had found a new love, a love which had even replaced soccer in his life. The love was given to him by a nurse early in his convalescence, and after he began propbing its many sweet mysteries, he was never again quite the same.

CHAPTER EIGHT

Not long after Julio returned home from the clinic, one of his father's nurses brought him a guitar. Apart from helping to keep him busy, she hoped it would encourage him to sit up, since getting him off his back was an important part of his recovery.

It was an inexpensive guitar, costing the equivalent of ten dollars, but it was an investment which proved to be worth its weight in diamonds.

At first, Julio would pick it up only to try and comfort himself after an unsuccessful "dispute" with his feet and legs. Rather than stew in anger and depression, he would go to the guitar—despite the fact that it weighed heavily against his chest and was bulky to handle in bed. He taught himself to play and made what he describes as "pleasant" sounds. "At least," he says, "the neighbors never complained." He also used it to keep track of how long he lay in bed, carving a notch in the instrument for every day he didn't get up and walk.

After a few weeks, Julio began to enjoy the guitar in its own right. He had the phonograph moved to his bedside so that he could play along with his collection of over two hundred records; after he had learned a few songs by ear, he would call in his mother and serenade her while she sat there knitting. Only rarely did he play for his father, whom he scared by hinting at just how important music was becoming to him. While strumming along with a radio broadcast from the annual Festival of San Remo, Julio remarked that one day he intended to sing in the festival. "It just came out from within me," he later explained, and all of a sudden his father grew "cold." What he'd heard in his son's voice was the same kind of affection the young man used to muster for athletics. But while soccer had a certain respectability and Dr. Iglesias had been able to accept that as an alternative to a diplomatic career for Julio, music worried him. The likelihood that Julio would be another Segovia or Paco de Lucia was remote, and he didn't care to think of his son earning a living in a bar or cabaret. Thus, for the time being, Rosario Iglesias remained her son's only fan.

But music appealed to Julio, and once he had gone through all of his own records, he borrowed records from friends and learned to love the music of Luis Gardey, of Jaime Morey, of Raphael and others. He also discovered foreign artists who were new to him, among them Paul Anka, Elvis Presley, the Beatles, and the Rolling Stones. Julio's musical horizons broadened, and as they did his enjoyment of music also increased.

Julio had always had a wonderful singing voice, though he'd never had the occasion or inclination to use it. Now, it may well have saved his sanity, for he was able to make the kind of progress on the guitar that he was unable to make with his legs. He progressed from notes to chords to melodies, and when singing along with records was no longer a challenge, he turned to composing.

In the beginning, Julio was not a prolific composer: the first song he ever wrote took him more than two years to complete, though it wasn't for lack of application. Rather, each successive draft failed to convey what Julio was trying to get across; that, despite setbacks, we must move forward; that, as the title itself says, *"La Vida Sigue Igual"*—"Life Continues All the Same."

Inarguably, "Life Continues All the Same" is Julio's favorite song, as well as being the most important composition of his life. Not only did it bind him tightly to music as a form of expression, but it was the first song he ever recorded. And, historically speaking, it was one thing more: a mirror of how Julio changed from week to week during his recuperation.

Julio acknowledges that "the song was for me more than for anybody else," though he adds that "it is also for those who want to be somebody in this world." In it, he counterpoints birth and death, laughter and tears, flood and drought, and concludes that in bad times as well as good, there is always a reason to fight for life. Not that the song was always so optimistic. Though he says today that he listens to it and does "not want to alter one single letter," in its early stages the song was more questioning than hopeful, more doubting than resolute. But as his mobility grew, Julio kept going back to the song until virtually every trace of despair had been replaced by a more encouraging tone. While it isn't a masterpiece of music by any means, the song *is* a moving expression of what Julio clearly felt was the most important quality in life: courage.

Early on in his recovery, Julio began to realize that music was replacing soccer as the love of his life. As ever, the tactile was one of his first clues. After the operation, he used to sit on the bed and run his soccer gear through his hands, "caressing the gloves, the jersey with its high neck, the knees, the white shin guards, the socks." He'd clutch one of the objects like an amulet, hoping some of its former magic might rub off on him. When he got the guitar, he found that he wanted the athletic gear less and less. The instrument was smooth and delicate, the strings taut and strong. Whether it was a matter of the tranquil replacing the aggressive, the future supplanting the past, or simply the fact that he could embrace the guitar as if it were a woman, Julio spent more time thinking about music and less about soccer.

Then, too, it's clear that soccer now rang a little hollow to him. Though Julio has said nothing more than "the goalkeeper just died," he reveals a great deal when discussing—rather vividly, at that—the writing of "Life Continues All the Same." He says, "I disemboweled it from myself, took the song from inside a little bit at a time, very slowly and with a certain pain." After an experience like that, stretched over a two-year period, the act of flying from post to post on the soccer field had to have lacked a certain dimension in his eyes.

Music gave Julio pleasure and release, and he pursued it with a deep sense of gratitude. But getting back on his feet was still his greatest preoccupation, and toward the middle of 1965 he took another major step toward that goal: trying to wean himself from the cane. It was, in many ways, the most difficult plateau of all; failure meant falling and having to struggle to stand up again time after time. Out of every hour of trying to walk without the cane, he spent most of that time getting up from the floor.

"I have fallen in other ways," says Julio, "physically and morally." Yet nothing was ever as difficult for him as the slow process of giving up the cane. He would sit on the edge of his bed, stand with the help of the cane, lay it aside when he was sure of his balance, take a step, and then drop. Pulling himself back on the bed, he'd start all over—and fall again. He never allowed anyone to help him, or to stand by as parents do with babies learning to walk. He wanted to do this by himself even, he admits, when there was a perpetual "look of terror on my face" as he anticipated each and every fall.

In time, though, he took his first step, then his second; his goal was "always to have more than yesterday, but less than tomorrow." He achieved that goal, and toward the end of the summer the handrails which had been fastened to walls along the hallway were removed and the cane was discarded. After nearly nineteen months of incapacitation, Julio Iglesias was walking again—haltingly, with stiff legs and at a snail's pace—but nonetheless *walking* by himself.

In the fall, Julio returned to Cambridge to resume his studies, and not long after that he resumed his love life as well. There, he met and fell in love with an eighteen-year-old woman named Gwendoline, whom he describes today as the most beautiful woman he has ever known, with "gorgeous wide cheekbones, blond hair, and gray eyes the color of steel."

The daughter of an exiled Russian aristocrat living in France, Gwendoline was the first woman that Julio ever truly loved. So intense was the love that, today, though he knows where Gwendoline is, he doesn't want to see her; he prefers the beautiful memories, which he says are "alive and fresh" in his mind, "like a rose in a vase with water." In fact, when their relationship ended due to his preoccupation with singing, his suffering was so great that it became the subject of one of his most moving and personal songs. Composed in 1970 for the Eurovision Festival in Holland, "Gwendoline" not only became one of the biggest hits of that year but also almost singlehandedly launched Julio's career outside of Spain. It's ironic that such triumph should come from such pain; yet, as Julio himself suggests in "Life Continues All the Same," it's the dark clouds which bring the life-giving rain.

Perhaps the only thing that affected Julio as much as Gwendoline was his official withdrawal from his other love, soccer. He did that by attending the first match he'd seen in years. He hadn't really wanted to go, not only because his instincts would still be to get out there and play, but also because the game symbolized a different Julio—a younger, more carefree, more superficial man, a Julio who drove too fast and had two-dimensional dreams. But he knew that going to the stadium was the only way to put that part of him behind. So he endured that valuable catharsis, which was akin to a wake, and he officially buried the past. Thereafter, Julio was able to attend soccer games solely as a spectator, which was how he now preferred it.

Being back at Cambridge was actually quite pleasant for Julio. It was the first significant change of scenery he'd had since the operation, and his attitude toward his studies was the best that it had ever been. He had matured, and he knew it. He also brought his music to England, where he and his roommates enjoyed hanging out in their room or in a park and singing in what was suddenly a very music-conscious Great Britain.

More than a year passed, during which time "Life Continues All the Same" remained unfinished. Finally, Antonio Villegas, one of Julio's roommates, heard him sing the song and urged him to complete it. Julio had a little trouble getting back into the song, but with constant encouragement from Antonio he hammered it into shape.

As the two of them sang the final version together in their room, little did either young man dream that less than a year later the song would be heard by millions of people across Spain. Without realizing it, Julio was, in his own words, "about to be born a third time."

CHAPTER NINE

Some things did not die in Julio during his convalescence. His ambition, for one. His need to be admired, for another. People who knew the torture he'd been through thought the world of him, of course, but that wasn't enough. It wasn't like the applause he used to get on the soccer field. He may not have needed goalkeeping any more, but he realized he needed attention, for people to sit up and take notice of what he'd done. And since "Life Continues All the Same" was something of which he was proud, he decided to try and get it before the public eye.

In his blissful naïveté, Julio returned home the following June, and immediately mailed the song to Columbia Records in Spain. In his covering letter, he said that he hoped the label might be interested in having one of their stars record it. As it turned out, they weren't. But since the powerful label *was* committed to developing new talent, and felt that "Life Continues All the Same" showed promise, they decided to submit it for competition at the Benidorm Song Festival.

This festival, held each year at the popular resort on the Mediterranean coast, was one of the most presti-

constant stimulant" that had evolved into "a hymn";
maybe Atonio saw it that way as well. Maybe others
would too.

When Julio finished the song, the crew made no
sign that *they* had been touched. There was perfunctory
chatter in the booth: they had gotten it all on tape, it
sounded fine, Julio could leave. But while the singer
smiled politely, he was in another world.

The song that I wrote is now a record. It's
permanent.

The reward had been worth the terror. Even the
days of awaiting the judges' response was sweet pain:
though he knew he would experience profound dejec-
tion if he were turned down, it was worth the risk. He
wanted to feel his spirits soar again, feel the emotional
high which came from knowing that his "hymn" meant
something to someone else.

It meant enough to the Benidorm panel to accept
it as part of their program. Julio got the word from a
Columbia executive, who told him that he'd have to be
in Benidorm the following night in order to check in.
He added that Julio would be making the four hundred
fifty kilometer drive with a young man named Manolo
Otero, a young singer with "a voice like Sinatra."
Columbia believed that Manolo had star quality—he
would, in fact, eventually become one of the top artists
in Spain—and they wanted to give his career a boost by
having him sing at the festival.

Julio was excited by the good news, and refused to
do more than take each moment as it came. The
thought of performing in public was so foreign that he
simply couldn't imagine how he'd feel: confident, like
he had felt on the soccer field, or petrified as he'd often
felt when he'd had to read a composition before his
classmates.

Picking his partner up early the next morning, Julio set out toward Benidorm. Their route carried them southeast through Don Quixote's immortal plains of La Mancha—a prophetic passage since one of Julio's early compositions, *"Quijote,"* is a metaphor for his own battles with windmills and giants.

The drive proved a suitable beginning for the crucible of Benidorm. It was a broiling summer day, and Julio's small car overheated constantly. "I don't remember how many stops we had to make along the road," Julio says, but he did find himself concluding early on that Quixote had had the right idea, traveling the road to glory by horse rather than by automobile.

It was early in the evening when the exhausted pair arrived at the beachside resort. The sun had not yet set and the beaches were still packed, and Julio glanced longingly at the sparkling waters of the Mediterranean. But Quixote wouldn't have paused to take a dip, and neither did Julio. Instead, they drove to the open-air amphitheater where the contest would take place.

Directed to the registration desk, Julio did not get quite the welcome he was expecting.

"Good evening, sir."

The portly official looked up from a notebook. "Yes?"

"We are Manolo Otero and Julio Iglesias."

"Who?"

"Otero and Iglesias," he repeated.

The balding man asked with a trace of impatience, "What *company* are you with?"

"Oh." Julio laughed, driving a palm against his forehead. "I'm sorry. We are with Columbia."

The executive ran his pencil down the list of names. "Ah yes, yes," he muttered, making a checkmark beside the entry. "Otero and Iglesias. Very good." He advised the pair that Julio was scheduled to rehearse with the band at nine the following morning, Otero early in the afternoon.

Both men thanked the official, and Otero turned to go. But Julio just stood there, smiling down at the official. The swarthy man lifted his eyes from the ledger.

"Was there something else?"

Rubbing his hands together, Julio asked softly, "I was wondering—that is, if you even *know*, sir—what time I will actually be performing."

"What *time*?"

"Yes," Julio said, choking and swallowing hard. "To sing my song. In what position on the schedule?"

The official referred back to his ledger, and without looking up informed Julio, "You sing first."

"First?" Julio gasped. No longer sure that he wanted to sing, he shook his head and said, "Oh, *shit!*"

"What did you say?" the beefy man shot back.

"Nothing," Otero cut in. "He's just overwhelmed by all of this."

"No—no, I *can't*," Julio continued, oblivious to his companion. "Couldn't you change my place? Maybe a little further down? You see, sir, this is the first time I'm singing in public, and I—"

"I'm sorry," the official said without conviction, "but the schedule has already been notarized. It cannot be changed."

Otero said, "Julio, the first in line casts his shadow across the rest. It's an honor."

The official added snootily, "Being first or last or anywhere in between is an honor. In any case, I certainly hope you show a little more enthusiasm and class onstage than you've shown me here."

"Of course," said the dazed Julio. "Enthusiasm and class . . ." he muttered as Otero led him away.

Julio followed slowly. He was still limping from the operation, a scar he carries to this day. Otero brought Julio back to reality by squeezing his shoulder and suggesting that if they hurried, they could check in and get to the beach while it was still light enough to see the girls.

Julio nodded and, coming around to his senses, smiled as he looked toward the beaches. The girls would be a breath of fresh air and, after that, maybe they would stop by at a nightclub or two. Reminding himself to take one moment at a time, Julio breathed deeply and increased his pace. He hasn't slowed down since.

CHAPTER TEN

J ulio rose early the following morning, going for a swim before breakfast. He ate little, his stomach doing flip-flops as he contemplated what he was about to do.

Heading to the pavilion, he was greatly comforted to learn that the singers who would be backing him up were La-la-la, popular Eurovision TV stars who, he says, "helped me a great deal. Just knowing they were behind me was a guarantee that the performance would achieve some level of success."

Much to his surprise, he was extremely calm during the rehearsal—at least for the first few minutes. After running through his song and feeling as though he'd done all right, he was crushed when the conductor shook his head and said to one of the judges, "Forget about the schedule. We're going to have to work with this guy." Casting a disgusted glance at Julio, he went on, "We're going to have to teach him how to keep tempo with an orchestra."

Julio's spirits withered, and during the two days before the actual competition, he logged twenty hours with the orchestra—learning how to listen for musical cues and how to stay in time with his backup singers. He also learned where to stand and even *how* to stand. By the time he was finished rehearsing, Julio felt certain he could do the routine in his sleep.

Julio's confidence was boosted considerably by the arrival of Enrique Garea from Columbia, a compassionate port in the storm! Yet, despite the handholding he received from Enrique during the day and a half of rehearsals, Julio found that he was anything but confident on the day of the festival. The unpressured feeling he'd taken away from the rehearsal was gone, blown away by the lights, by the crowds, by the radio trucks, by the reporters milling about, by the fact that this was all happening at night, which was when all the really first-class entertainment ceremonies were held.

Dressed in a white suit, Julio walked with Otero toward the arena. Though Otero said he was nervous, he didn't seem to be; the fact that Julio was trembling openly made him feel all the more inadequate. As they walked from the hotel, Julio looked up at the sky. The stars were bright and the night was hot and muggy, wiltingly so; he was already perspiring, and hoped no one would notice it up on the stage. He had experienced many humid nights like this in nearby Peniscola, but never in a suit and tie, getting ready to perform for several million people. The closer they got to the stadium, the more terrified he became.

He wished it were all over and that he was lying on the beach at Peniscola, shoes off, his feet digging up the sand. His parents were there on the annual Iglesias vacation, and he would be joining them immediately after the festival. They knew nothing about where he was or what he was doing; he didn't think his father would have approved, and decided not to tell him rather than have to disobey him.

The preparations that took place before he went on are a blur in Julio's mind: people running around checking lights and wires, the hum of the audience in the background.

While last-minute details were being ironed out, Enrique came up behind his two charges and wished them well. Otero thanked him and Julio did likewise, though he seemed a little pale.

"Are you all right?" Enrique inquired.

"Fine," Julio said quietly. "Just a little frightened, I guess."

"You'll get over it," Enrique assured him. "If not," he teased, "I may have to return with you to Cambridge. I'm counting on you, Julio."

Just then the announcer took the stage, and while he was welcoming everyone to the festival, Julio suddenly felt that there was no way he could go through with this. His legs and feet were like concrete, and refused to budge. Getting his big toe to move when he was bedridden had been easier than this.

The announcer paused and studied a piece of paper he was holding. "The first song," he said, "is entitled 'Life Continues All the Same.' The words and music are by Julio Iglesias, and the composer himself will sing the song."

The announcer stepped back and the audience began to applaud, but Julio just stood there.

"Go ahead," Enrique urged, "you're on."

Julio looked down at his dead legs. He noticed that his pants were too short and wondered if he should go back to the room and change into his other suit.

Otero asked, "Julio, are you all right?"

Julio nodded, but he still couldn't move. A minute passed, and the announcer looked over. Enrique motioned for him to be patient, then turned to Julio.

"You can't do this, Julio. You can't back out now."

"I won't," he said, his voice barely above a whisper. "I just need a minute. That's all, just a minute."

"You've already *taken* a minute!" Enrique squealed. "What do you want, *another* one?"

"Yes," Julio said, "one more would be nice."

Exasperated, Enrique waited. Two minutes passed, and then three. Finally, the executive just pursed his lips and, stepping behind Julio, literally pushed him onto the stage. The lanky young man stumbled into the spotlight, quickly regaining his balance and walking mechanically to center stage. He couldn't see anyone in the audience because the lights were too bright, but he knew they were out there, staring at him. He had their attention; now all he had to do was excel at something he'd never done before.

There was no guitar this time, nothing to hold, so Julio awkwardly slipped his hands into his pockets. "Then music started," he says, "and it sounded good. And I thought, *Dear God, that's mine!*" His song, his anthem. For a brief moment before he was to join in, Julio was transported to his bed in Madrid, to the time he'd assured his father that one day he would sing in a song festival.

Was that only braggadocio? he asked himself. Could he really do it? And what about that sweet pain of giving something your all and waiting to see if it had been enough? Didn't he have the backbone for that kind of pressure?

Something clicked at that instant, and Julio reached inside for his voice. "It came from deep within me," he remembers, "from my testicles, my liver, my soul." His hands came out as he "found a pocket in my heart," and he started to sing.

All through the day, Julio had worried about what

he would do if he forgot the words or got ahead of the band or if the microphone suddenly went dead. But none of those things happened, and when he finished he was astonished to hear people applauding. He thanked them and bowed slightly, then hurried into the wings.

Otero came over and threw his arms around Julio, hugging him tightly; Enrique, self-satisfied, told him he'd done a superb job. Other faces drifted past, voices floating over, congratulating him. At first, Julio thought the compliments were from people who had taken pity on him. But the more he heard, the more convinced he became that he'd actually done a good job.

Relieved and feeling so good that he didn't care whether he won the contest or not, Julio listened to the other acts, which included his friend Otero. He applauded his friend heartily and, having been on that stage, admired all the more not only Otero's voice but his style.

The festival lasted several days, and at 11:30 P.M. on July 18, 1968, the winner was announced.

It was Julio.

"I was astonished," he says of the moment he heard his name called out. For a long moment, once again, he couldn't move, only this time he didn't need Enrique to snap him out of it. All it took was the applause. He strode onto the stage to claim his trophy and the prize of one hundred fifty thousand pesetas, the equivalent of three thousand dollars. He thanked the judges, embraced Otero and Enrique, and was immediately swarmed by reporters. One of them, Raul Matas of Channel 13 in Chile, would later become one of Julio's close friends; he is the only person in the world who owns a copy of Julio's original, crude Columbia recording of "Life Continues All the Same," a record which he has refused to sell despite being offered what Julio describes as "handfuls of money."

After the newspaper, radio, and TV reporters had besieged him, Julio returned to the hotel and celebrated the night away. Early the following morning, without having had a wink of sleep, Julio went with photographers through the streets of Benidorm, posing for pictures which would appear in all the nation's magazines and newspapers.

While he was en route to becoming the Benidorm poster boy, Julio happened to bump into one of the festival's many celebrity attendees, his old idol Ricardo Zamora. Introducing himself to the soccer legend, Julio burbled, "You see what I've done, Don Ricardo? Well, it was *your* example that enabled me to do this. I couldn't achieve it in soccer, so I'm going to be as good as you are—only in music."

The goalie was flattered and Julio impulsively hugged the star; the award and prize money notwithstanding, that meeting was the highlight of Benidorm for Julio.

When the photographers were through, Julio made arrangements to meet with Columbia back in Madrid, then climbed in his car for the drive to Peniscola. He drove with the radio turned up loud, singing at the top of his lungs. He doesn't remember if the car overheated that day; chances are good he wouldn't have cared even if it had.

Arriving late in the day at the summer house in Peniscola, he left the trophy in his suitcase and all but skipped inside. His parents would have read the newspaper by now; he couldn't wait to see the expressions on their faces.

"Hello!" he shouted as he walked inside. His mother answered from the kitchen, and Julio strutted in. She smiled sweetly and kissed him on the cheek, then returned to preparing dinner; his father looked up from a book and asked him how the drive had been.

Julio couldn't believe they hadn't heard; this had to be some kind of game.

"Father," he said, "didn't you hear the news?"

"What news?" Dr. Iglesias inquired. His perplexity seemed sincere, and Julio plucked the morning newspaper from the table, waving it at arm's length.

"Didn't you read about Benidorm?"

"I don't understand, Julio. Read *what* about Benidorm?"

"About the top prize going to Julio Iglesias?"

His father stared at him and his mother turned around. There was a long silence, after which she said, "We read that someone named Julio Iglesias had won, but we didn't think—"

"Yes!" Julio shouted, jabbing his chest. "Yes, it was *this* Julio Iglesias! Not someone else's Julio. It was *me!*"

Still not sure that they were convinced, the young man pulled the one hundred fifty thousand pesetas from his pocket and laid them on the table. His parents looked from the money to their son with disbelief, after which his mother hugged him and began to cry. His father also congratulated their boy, though he was less enthusiastic than Julio would have liked. But the young singer knew how his father felt about music, and so Julio took his relative indifference in stride. He also knew that deep inside the elder Iglesias respected accomplishment, and this had to rank among the most miraculous in recent memory.

Besides, while his reception here hadn't been quite what he expected, there was someone else with whom Julio wanted to share his triumph. He had been going out with Gwendoline for several months now, and he asked his parent's permission to fly to Paris to be with her on this momentous occasion.

His father considered his son, and after a moment said with a faint smile, "It's your prize money. Enjoy it."

Julio thanked him and embraced his mother, then ran to the car to get the trophy. After showing it to his parents, he hurriedly repacked it and, bidding them good-bye, drove to the airport in Madrid. Julio booked passage on the first flight to Paris and, after calling Gwendoline to give her the good news, collapsed into a plastic seat in the waiting room.

This process of being reborn was tiring, he decided. First learning to walk, then making the radical change from soccer player to singer. He vowed to make this new phase of his life a spectacular one, if for no other reason than it was getting tougher and tougher to snuggle into a phoenix suit.

If he could have known just how spectacularly he was to succeed, even Julio Iglesias would have been amazed.

CHAPTER ELEVEN

Gwendoline met Julio at the airport, and the two spent a delightful time in Paris Julio likes nothing more than to share his successes with someone else, and Gwendoline was a rapt, loving partner.

With the prize money burning a hole in his pocket, Julio flew with Gwendoline back to Galicia for a visit They had a pleasant few days, after which Gwendoline returned to Paris and Julio went back to Madrid. In the days that followed, the couple spent hours on the phone, lonely and frustrated at being apart. They began discussing marriage, but that's all they would ever do: "Something was happening to me," Julio says. "A spark had been struck, the taste of success; and a giant was born in me. The giant of music."

As Columbia sifted through the fallout from Benidorm—including countless requests from artists who wished to record "Life Continues All the Same" —it became clear that they had a hit in the person of Julio Iglesias. The company called him in, signed him to a contract, had him cut his own recording of "Life Continues All the Same," and asked if he had any other

songs to record. Julio admitted that he hadn't, and
Columbia told him to write some quick: they wanted an
album's worth of songs ready to record in October.

Flabbergasted, Julio found himself in a dilemma.
Columbia stipulated that once the album had been
released, they wanted him free to do concerts to promote the record, which all but precluded returning to
Cambridge. That was fine with Julio—though, not surprisingly, it was considerably less than fine with his
father.

Though Julio was sure of himself and emphatic
when the two men sat down to discuss it, Dr. Iglesias
was too practical to see past the awesome obstacles that
stood before his son. "It's the wrong road," he said after
hearing Julio out. "This singing is sheer nonsense."

Julio didn't agree, of course, noting that Benidorm
had given him a formidable leg up on a musical career.
However, he was willing to compromise. In exchange
for his father's blessings and two years to prove himself,
Julio promised that if he didn't make it in that time, he
would give up music and return to his studies.

"I won't lie to you and say it doesn't matter," Julio
confessed. "You know what music has come to mean to
me, and I can't let this opportunity pass me by. I just
can't."

To his credit, Dr. Iglesias said that while he still
didn't approve of Julio's plans, he would help him in
any way he could. The young man was jubilant, and
cleared his mind of everything but the task that lay
before him.

During the weeks that followed, Julio spent every
day and night on the balcony of the house, writing
more songs. With inspired haste he composed the likes
of "No Ilores, Mi Amor," "Yo Canto," "El Viejo Pablo,"
"Lagrimas Tiene al Camino," "Alguien en Algún Lugar,"

and others. They were simple songs, all of them, about life and love and "the web of regrets" everyone has. He hadn't the time or interest to be profound. Julio only wanted to touch people. As he later said, "My songs are very simple... without sophistication or intellectual pretension. Perhaps that's why so many people recognize themselves in my songs."

In the midst of this creative outpouring, Julio's single of "Life Continues All the Same" was released and shot to number one. Instead of feeling pure triumph, however, Julio found himself challenged and pressured. It was the same feeling he'd had during hs convalescence, when he refused to take one step less than the day before. If his album weren't as successful, not only might the industry regard him as a has-been, a one-hit wonder, but he would consider himself a failure. Without a doubt, twenty-five-year-old Julio Iglesias was the unhappiest number-one recording artist in musical history.

Because there was so much riding on the work, and because he was so close to it, Julio would frequently become anxious about what he was writing. "Life Continues All the Same" had taken two years to hatch, and now he was supposed to compose brilliance on a timetable, nearly a dozen songs in just over two months. Sometimes he became overly critical, fighting with a lyric or melody until he threw down the pencil in disgust. Sometimes he feared he wasn't being critical *enough* and discarded a tune or line that had come too easily. More often than he liked, he would find himself thinking that the first song had been a fluke, that he would never again achieve that level of inspiration or artistry.

To keep up his spirits as well as his objectivity, Julio made frequent visits to Columbia, where the experts would look the material over. Whatever seemed misdirected or unfinished was put on the back burner; the rest was critiqued so that Julio could fine-tune it. To his credit, Julio never became insecure when his songs were given low marks: he simply grasped at the positive, delighted to learn that some of the work *was* good, that "Life Continues All the Same" hadn't been a flash in the pan.

But if the time he spent at Columbia worked wonders for his creative juices, it did even more for Julio's other driving force, his libido. Throughout August and early September, Julio would call Gwendoline every day. But as he became more involved in the record world, he discovered that there were beautiful young women everywhere he turned, from singers to Columbia staff members to reporters to the industry's many warm bodies and hangers-on. They weren't a crackling voice on the end of a long-distance line, but very real and very desirable; in no time flat Julio's interest in Gwendoline became diluted, and he stopped calling her every day. After a while, he stopped calling her at all.

Today Julio is ashamed of his behavior, and is quick to cry *mea culpa*. He also chastises himself for waiting until the following spring before officially ending the relationship. He did it in May, stopping at Gwendoline's house unnanounced as he returned home from the Debrasow Festival in Romania. While she was surprised to see him, she seemed "distant" throughout the evening of small talk. Julio had half-expected that kind of reception and, though her aloofness hurt, it made the parting that much easier.

Yet Julio insists it wasn't the parade of women that killed their love. It was music. "What I wished and desired above all things," he says succinctly, "was to sing." The women were just lovely diversions but music was a passion, especially during those two hectic months of composing when Julio poured his heart into his guitar. There simply wasn't anything left to give to Gwendoline.

Little did he know that the debacle with Gwendoline was just a taste of the devastating impact his career would have on his relationships with women. The worst was yet to come.

By October, Julio had completed his ten songs and Columbia sent him to London to record them. He was mystified at being sent abroad: the Decca studios were among the finest in the world, and only the biggest names in music recorded there. But Columbia knew what it was doing. "Life Continues All the Same" had been recorded by various artists and was the number-one song in Spain and in several Central and Latin American countries. Julio's presence at the Decca studios would underscore the fact that Columbia considered him to be a Very Important Artist. Then as now, hype was as important as talent to the success of an artist.

Nonetheless, the tactic had just the opposite effect on Julio. Instead of feeling proud and lofty, he was awed and humbled to be cutting his record at the studio where the Beatles had recorded their classic albums. Only Julio's innate drive enabled him to overcome that impasse: whether it was Ricardo Zamora or the Beatles, rather than remain intimidated, he shifted his ego into high and strove to equal their standards of excellence.

At the time, the music industry was a fairly standardized one; recordings by Spanish balladeers possessed something of a cookie-cutter quality. Spain's music had come to the region centuries before by way of invading Arabs, whose culture was a patchwork of Greek and Persian influences. As a result, Spanish

songs tend to be both stormy and emotional, leaning
toward the minor key and fraught with complex progressions and jumps in the music. It is easy music to do
badly, and only the true virtuosos become successful.

The musical tradition in which Julio was trying to
carve a niche consists primarily of two types of singing:
cante jondo, which is very low and very downbeat; and
cante flamenco, which is spirited to the point of near-
madness. As a result, listeners either danced to a voice
that was percolating with glee or drowning in sorrow—
there was no middle ground. Singers actually had a lot
of the tradition of the bullfighters in them, posturing
handsomely but, for all their flourishes, performing in a
fairly ritualistic manner.

Given this vogue, Julio could not have accomplished what the Beatles had done: upended conven-
tion and introduced a new form of expression. Nor did
he care to. Julio's objective was solely to perform as
well as the other balladeers and sell enough records to
get invited back into the studio.

Yet while Julio didn't realize it, he couldn't have
been like the other balladeers. He lacked their classical, often exhaustive training, so that instead of singing
from the example of others, he sang from the heart.
And that worked to his advantage. While his voice was
not as strong as those of his contemporaries, it had a
way of wrapping itself around a word or phrase to make
it real. Other singers intellectualized emotions, playing
to the audience's expectations; Julio internalized a song.
Rather than *complaining* about a lost love or squandered
life he actually seemed to *feel* them, and that proved to
be the heart of his appeal.

But before he could appeal to anyone he had to sell
records, and in that regard he had a very important ace
in the hole: "Life Continues All the Same." The song

was so well-known that even if the album had been indistinguishable from anything else on the market, people would have picked it up just to see what else this Julio Iglesias could write. As it turned out, the record-buying public liked what they heard, and did more than just insure Julio a return trip to the studio. They quickly made his debut album a number-one hit.

Naturally, Julio immediately began to fear that maybe that album had been a fluke, that his next album couldn't possibly be as successful without "Life Continues All the Same" to help it along.

Fortunately, Julio didn't have a lot of free time to dwell on the future. Columbia told him to pack his bags and handed him an airplane ticket to Chile. He may have had a hit in Spain, but there was a large Spanish-speaking world out there and Columbia wanted to make sure that it knew all about Julio Iglesias.

CHAPTER TWELVE

The Viña del Mar song festival is something of a musical Miss Universe pageant, a face-off of winners from music festivals around the world.

Most nominees in any awards contest prattle about it being an honor "just to be nominated," but for Julio it was the truth. Most of the people against whom he was competing had studied music and had actively pursued it as a career. For him to have won would have been something more than a miracle, and he decided ahead of time that this would not be a competition but a learning experience, a chance to study other young singers and to gauge how they reacted to him.

To prepare his ego for the inevitable, Julio tried to insure that on the trip over, at least, he got his share of adulation. Rather than check his guitar at the gate, he brought it on board and strummed his way to Chile. It was a simpler time, and people were enchanted rather than annoyed; then, too, he was traveling coach, where his music was lost amid the noise and cramped confusion of the cabin. Only a few people asked if he was a musician and, when informed that he was the composer

of "Life Continues All the Same," were mildly impressed.
No one asked for his autograph, though, which both
surprised the young man and put him in his place. He
wondered if he'd have fared better telling them that he
used to play soccer for Real Madrid. . . .

Viña del Mar more than made up for whatever
disappointment he felt during the passage. Not many
celebrities passed through the Pudahuel Airport, and
the arriving singers were welcomed like royalty. Girls
gathered and screamed convulsively at every singer
who appeared, and photographers and reporters mobbed
the contestants.

"I was a relative unknown," Julio quips, "barely
known by my own record company." But Chile made
him feel like a superstar, from the press conference at
the airport to the first-class accommodations.

The open-air arena where the festival was held was
considerably larger than the one in Benidorm, and Julio
was more nervous than he'd expected. He sang "timidly
but elegantly," as he describes it, and though Julio did
not take home the festival's top prize he was overjoyed
not to have embarrassed himself in the presence of
some truly accomplished competition.

Besides, Julio did take home one very special
prize. While he was walking the streets of the city, a
young girl approached him, a beautiful "Lolita with
splendid legs and very large eyes," and asked for his
autograph. As they spoke, he realized that she had not
stopped him because he had been in a contest but
because his song had meant something to her. "From
that moment on," says Julio, "I have never stopped
loving my fans. Many of my colleagues don't do them
justice, but they are more than necessary for an artist.
They're your keepers. They follow you with the preci-

sion of a detective and the love of a mother, and the
doors of my heart are always open to them."

Toward the end of their brief talk, Julio was amazed
to find that this girl was just one of many fans he would
be leaving behind in Chile. Before leaving the country,
he had actually sanctioned his first fan club, a prize
which was greater than any the festival could have
accorded him.

The remainder of 1969 proved to be an eye-opener
for Julio, a harbinger of what was to come. It seemed to
him that he was always on the road, both in Spain and
abroad, and he quickly purged himself of the notion
that the life of a singer was a glamorous one.

After returning from Chile, he and a group of four
back-up musicians went to fairs throughout Spain, *ferias*
like the one he had attended the night of his accident.
Starting at the Mediterranean city of Valencia, they
moved north and were well-received at each stop as
Julio performed the songs from his album. Not every
stop was ideal: sometimes the group wasn't paid and
had to sleep on park benches as well as go hungry; even
when they *did* sleep in hotels, they often shared their
beds with bedbugs "the size of elephants." The tour
was an important lesson in humility for Julio.

Following the tour, he took a crash course in
Romanian, since his next stop was the Debrasow Festival in Romania. Not only did he have to learn the words
to his songs and a few phrases of greeting, he had to
relearn the *cadence* of the songs. It wasn't just a matter
of fitting another language into his standard Spanish
delivery. Romanian—like Italian, French, Japanese, English, and other languages Julio would one day master—
had its own emphasis and rhythm, both of which Julio
had to learn if he were to be effective. And learn them

he did, appearing on national TV and winning the hearts of his hosts. Julio was gratified, but Columbia was delighted: in just a few months Julio had gone from an unknown to a budding international star.

It's likely that the afterglow of his resounding success was one of the reasons Julio had stopped to see Gwendoline on his way home. Not only was he preoccupied with his career, but his newfound ability to stir people through music—especially to arouse women with a word or a glance—had to make it difficult for him to enjoy relatively mundane, old-fashioned love. He was a human aphrodisiac, and he had to be free to spread that around, literally as well as emotionally.

Hard upon his return, Julio was shipped to Guatemala at the behest of the Red Cross. Though Central America regularly hosted Spanish artists, Julio felt privileged to be there and made that plain onstage and off. His sincerity won him the love of that country as well, and a second international audience had been established.

Carrying his musical argosy to a third front, Julio undertook his greatest challenge to date: trying to establish a foothold in fickle, demanding Italy. Nor was it a minor-league fair at which he'd be appearing, but the important San Remo Festival—the one at which he told his father he'd one day sing.

The trip to Italy meant a crash course in Italian, and Julio made a supreme effort to become as fluent as possible. He also listened to Italian records in order to pick up the subtleties that singers used to "sell" those songs. While Julio would refine his language skills over the years, he made enough of an impression on the natives so that he wasn't hooted off the stage. In Italy, that was the equivalent of having a fan club.

Later that summer Julio was back on the road in

Spain, after which he embarked on one of the most unusual projects of his career: filming a newsreel-like autobiography.

Columbia and a Spanish film company collaborated to produce the "pseudodocumentary" entitled—what else?—*Life Continues All the Same*, in which Julio re-created the important events of the last three years. He felt a horrible chill as stunt drivers re-created the crash, and felt uneasier still when he returned to the clinic where he and his doctors simulated the operation for the cameras.

Yet the most difficult part of the film for Julio was donning his Real Madrid uniform and playing himself "before" the accident. His reflexes were rusty but looked great on film, and he smiled as though he were having the time of his life. But inside he was hurting. Unlike Gwendoline, the soccer ball bore him no grudges and welcomed him back unjudgmentally. He missed the activity, the physical competition—missed it more than he had realized. But like any first love, fanning the embers brought warmth without raising a fire. In soccer, the audience was merely a spectator. In music, they were a part of it. One brought adulation, the other inspired love. He was beyond that self-centered lifestyle, and the experience left him with a tearful, bittersweet aftertaste.

The motion picture played before the main feature in movie theaters around Spain, used as a promotional tool wherever he was soon to appear or, conversely, was unable to perform. In a perverse way, Julio was lucky that his recent life had been so dramatic: what would have been melodramatic and downright narcissistic under ordinary circumstances played just right with the empathetic public, and helped to stimulate interest in the singer.

One of the paradoxes which has plagued Julio throughout his career is that despite the credit that people give him for bravely fighting his paralysis and then boldly tackling one of the most difficult professions on earth, he has never wanted for anything. He had the finest medical attention during his convalescence, and he never went hungry while establishing himself as an artist. Even if he had fallen, his parents were always there to pick him up.

Julio has long since stopped apologizing for having lived a life of relative privilege. Yet, as if in answer to his critics, he has always gone out of his way to dwell on the pain in his life—perhaps not even consciously, much of the time. But pain is never far from his thoughts.

The most dramatic example of that is something he did late in the summer of 1969. Winning a song festival in Barcelona, Julio was accorded the privilege of representing his country in Eurovision, the European song festival to be held the following year in Holland.

Rather than play it safe and sing a proven crowd-pleaser with the eyes of all Europe upon him, he got in a car with his cousin Ramón and drove to his uncle's house in Galicia. There, Julio composed one of the most extraordinary songs of his career: "Gwendoline."

It wasn't easy. He had made peace with himself over what had happened; by writing the song, he was accepting the psychological burden of reliving her love and his own insensitivity in every concert he gave. The public wouldn't know that, of course. They would hear the anguish in his voice, and hurt along with him, but the song was not a blatant confessional. However, it was important to Julio that he do this, that he roll up his emotional sleeves and suffer. It was necessary if he were to be true to his art; more importantly, it was necessary for his own self-respect. He had to prove to himself and to the world that a patrician lifestyle did not mean he had a heart of stone.

The fact that "Gwendoline" not only became the hit of Eurovision but also reached the top of the charts throughout Europe showed just how effectively he achieved his goal. The fact that the song still touches Julio shows just how precisely he evoked his pain, and how that first great love also still warms him. As he was moved to write in his 1981 autobiography, *Between Heaven and Hell*, "If I have not told you before thank you very much, Gwendoline. Thank you again, my dear Gwendoline."

CHAPTER THIRTEEN

For the most part, 1970 was as much a blur of airports and tour stops as 1969.

In addition to Holland, Julio performed at a festival in Cannes, at another in Luxembourg, and struggled to learn the rudiments of a third foreign language, Japanese, before flying to the Osaka Festival. It's a very different, very difficult language for a Westerner to learn, and rather than flatter the locals all he did was amuse them with his phonetic, often incomprehensible Japanese. His album was already getting recognition in the country, and the Japanese couldn't understand why the Spaniard simply hadn't let himself be Spanish.

But Julio refused to do "merely" what was expected of him. He believed that being a good guest in another land was as important as being a good entertainer, and he continued to work on his Japanese. Today, while he is not as fluent in Japanese as he is in other languages, he sings his lyrics and engages in patter with ease and precision. Each new Julio Iglesias album sells over two million copies in Japan, which is more records than most native artists sell.

Unfortunately, Julio had even more trouble during

his first trip to North America. Singing at the Montmartre Cabaret in Miami, he happened to mention that his songs were well-liked in Cuba—an innocent but inappropriate boast which shocked the many anti-Castro members of his audience. It would take years for Julio to live the comment down, and he has since been careful to avoid any kind of political statements in his concerts. If the U.S. in 1970 was something of a low point in his career—though not a failure, by any means, for he received a valuable education about the country and its people—his concert in Puerto Banus, Spain, was a high water mark. The presence of Princess Grace of Monaco brought out the Prince Charming in Julio, and he gave one of his most poised and stylish performances to date. He was learning and he was growing, not only in ability but in ambition: the more confident he became, the grander his goals became.

Like the archetypal adventurer, he took on challenges "because they were there." He broke a long-standing national record by performing forty-one concerts in forty-one cities in a single month, and by early the following year watched his album climb past the million-seller mark. He resumed his conquest of Japan in 1971 by boldly returning to the country and recording one of his songs there, "Como el Alamo al Camino," becoming a hit as "Anatamo Uramo"; barely pausing for breath, he participated in an important song festival in Knokke, Belgium, after which he made his first trips to Mexico, Puerto Rico, and Panama.

Everywhere Julio appeared, record sales skyrocketed and fan clubs blossomed; by 1972, Julio Iglesias had not only reached the goal he'd set for himself, to *survive* as a singer, but he had also won an award from Columbia for selling more records worldwide than any artist in their roster. Julio hadn't simply "arrived." He had conquered.

But there was one field he had yet to conquer, and that was love. He had openly regretted letting Gwendoline go, and though he had a platonic girlfriend, an actress in London, she didn't fill him the way he yearned to be filled.

The loneliness hit him hardest when he was off the road and idle, and it was during one of these layovers in May of 1970 that he met his future wife.

Julio was invited to a party being given by longtime friend Juan, one at which many of their old chums would be present. He went, anxious to catch up on what everyone had been doing while he was on tour.

One of the friends-of-a-friend who had also been invited was a young Philippine student named Isabel Preysler. She was an exotic-looking eighteen-year-old, one who absolutely "enchanted" Julio with "her beauty; her big eyes, which were very mysterious; her style; her lovely skin."

It was not Julio's way just to walk over to a woman someone else had brought and start talking to her: he wanted to be properly introduced. It was the way of his social class, particularly if the woman was as cultured as this one seemed to be.

Unfortunately, circumstance prevented the meeting from happening that night, and Julio subsequently voiced his regrets to Juan and another of his close friends, Ayesa.

"Well," Ayesa said and shrugged, "I guess that means you'll just have to join us this weekend at the *feria* at Casa de Campo."

"What do you mean?" Julio inquired.

"There's going to be a party during the feast," said Ayesa, "and she'll probably be there."

"How do you know?" Julio pressed.

Juan answered, "Because her friends will be there, and she goes where they go." Heartened, Julio arranged with Juan to introduce him before he did anything else, and found himself looking forward to Saturday night with unusual anticipation.

It was a sweltering June evening, and no one was hotter under the collar than Julio. He stood in a corner of the apartment and sipped a glass of wine to stay calm, but his heart began to race all the same when Isabel arrived. She was dressed in a satin sari, at once fetching and innocent, and part of Julio just wanted to stand there and stare as if she were a priceless museum piece.

True to his word, the instant Juan saw Isabel enter the room he scurried over and ushered Julio to her side.

"Forgive me," he said to the young woman once her girlfriends had left her, "but the other night, at my party, I was unable to introduce you to a friend of mine, a friend who was *very* anxious to meet you." He grinned, proudly slapping Julio on the shoulders. "Isabel Preysler, I would like you to meet my dear friend Julio . . . Julio *Iglesias*, the famous singer."

Isabel smiled politely and Julio bowed his head. "I'm sorry," she said when their eyes met, "but I don't listen to much music. What do you sing?"

"What does he sing?" Juan huffed. "Everyone in Spain has heard of Julio Iglesias, the winner at Beni—"

"It's all right," Julio interrupted. "I'm sure Miss Preysler is quite busy with her studies."

"He wrote 'Life Continues All the Same'!" Juan went on. "And if you haven't heard it, you should. It's a brilliant song, a classic."

Isabel nodded. "Yes, I *have* heard that song. As I recall, it's very lovely."

"Thank you," Julio replied softly.

Smiling sweetly, Isabel looked from Julio to Juan and then glanced around at the other partygoers.

Juan broke the silence by excusing himself, then winked at Julio as he walked away. Julio thanked him and, after getting Isabel something to drink, spent the good part of an hour telling her who he was and listening intently as she spoke about her home and her studies.

The evening passed pleasantly, Julio spending little time with Isabel after their initial conversation. He didn't want to crowd her and, besides, he knew he would have her all to himself after the party: by prearrangement, he had agreed to act as chauffeur to everyone who lived in Isabel's part of town. He would make certain that wherever he had to drive, her home would be the last stop.

Julio looked forward to the end of the evening with the keen expectation of a child counting the hours until Christmas morning. And when the crowd began to disperse not long before dawn, Julio began to assemble his group.

When everyone was together and had given Julio their addresses, he studied the list and announced, "All right. We'll drop off Manuela first, and then José—"

"No," Isabel said curtly, "that makes no sense. The most direct route is to go past my house, then take the others home."

Julio's spirits fell but, rather than make a fuss, he settled for walking Isabel to the door of her building. Asking for her telephone number, he was told, "It won't serve you any purpose," since she was about to return to the Philippines to visit with family.

After extracting a promise that she'd call him when she returned to Spain, Julio fell into a deep depression. Even though it was obvious to him that Isabel wasn't as smitten with him as he was with her, he resolved not to give up on her.

Because he was about to record his second album, Julio barely had time to obtain Isabel's telephone number from Juan before flying to London. In the days that followed he was too busy to call, and when he finally got around to it he expected to learn that she had already left for home.

Much to Julio's surprise, not only did Isabel answer the phone, but she admitted that the story about the Philippines had been a sham. Julio was puzzled, unable to decide if she'd been playing hard to get, or whether he'd done something to put her off. It would be years before he discovered the truth; in the meantime, all that mattered was that Isabel was sufficiently impressed by his tenacity that she agreed to go out with him the following week.

The thought of Isabel preoccupied Julio almost as much as his work. It was a feat no person or event had accomplished for nearly two years, and more than once he sat back and tried to fathom exactly what it was about Isabel that appealed to him. Her beauty and poise were a part of it, of course, but he suspected that it was her attitude which attracted him the most. She was aloof without being arrogant, with an Oriental sense of tranquility. Julio found these qualities alluring; no doubt he also found them challenging. Like every goal in Julio's life, the more difficult it was to attain the more he wanted it. He was obviously convinced that a wellspring of love and devotion lay behind Isabel's beautiful exterior, and he intended to experience it.

It seemed more like a month than a week, but

Julio eventually finished the album and found himself back in Spain, introducing himself to the servant who answered the door.

Isabel seemed a little friendlier than before, and they had a delightful night dining and then dancing. As Julio describes it, "Everything went as anticipated. That is, nothing happened." But when he saw her to the door, he did sense that "a fire had started" between them, and she agreed to see him again. Within a few weeks, unless Julio were on the road, he and Isabel were getting together each and every day.

Despite the time they spent together, the relationship was a lopsided one for quite some time. Isabel liked Julio, but she was not as committed to him as he was to her. Countless times he would wonder why, but it would be years before he discovered the truth: that she disliked what he did for a living. The fact that he was a singer, an artist, was what had put her off the night they met, and it remained a hurdle throughout their courtship and marriage.

Isabel has never said exactly *why* she objected to Julio's career, though it isn't difficult to figure out. On the one hand, Isabel is a very private person who didn't like seeing her lover making a public spectacle of himself. More significant, however, is the fact that for all the love Julio genuinely had for Isabel, his passion for music sustained its peak levels over the years.

Isabel's instincts had told her that Julio wasn't for her. She had fought these emotions back because she liked being with him, and clearly never intended to fall in love with him. But she did fall for him and her resentment proved to be a time bomb more potent than even she could have realized.

CHAPTER FOURTEEN

"**I** owe many things to Isabel. Never have I lived with such intensity, with such love. But I have said it many times, that I will sing until the end of my days. And no one or anything is going to stop me in what I want, in what I am."

A decade later, Julio accepts much of the blame for what would happen between him and Isabel. But in September of 1970, Isabel was the most important thing in his life. He "declared" himself to her, and when he was touring in October he reaffirmed his love each night over the phone. The size of the phone bills didn't matter: even if he hadn't been making "more money than I ever dreamed I could," he would have called. He needed that personal contact and instant gratification. To this day, Julio hasn't the patience to write a letter; he has sixteen telephones in his Florida home and, not surprisingly, his phone bill each month averages fifty thousand dollars.

Appropriately enough, it was over the phone that Julio first proposed to Isabel. He remembers that when he asked for her hand, "although my voice was very sure, my legs were not."

JULIO!

Lady Killer AP/Wide World Photos

Julio performs during a special tribute to Bob Hope in honor of Hope's 80th birthday.

Julio and Bob Hope at Coca-Cola press conference in 1984.
UPI/Bettmann Archive

Julio with Johnny Carson on "The Tonight Show."
UPI/Bettmann Archive

Julio, Andy Williams and Leslie Uggams join the Reagans
for a special "Christmas in Washington" show in 1983.
UPI/Bettmann Archive

Michael Jackson's sister, La Toya, with Julio and Beach Boys lead singer, Mike Love, at a July 4th concert.

Julio and Mike Love in action. AP/Wide World Photos

Diana Ross and Julio. The Howard Frank Collection

The famous duo: Julio and Willie Nelson. AP/Wide World Photos

Raquel Welch
and Julio.

UPI/Bettmann Archive

Julio hugs
Phyllis Diller at
an American
Cancer Society
Benefit.
AP/Wide World Photos

Julio receiving the famous "Diamond Disc" award from Paris mayor Jacques Chirac and Norris McWhirter, editor of GUINNESS BOOK OF WORLD RECORDS.

UPI/Bettmann Archive

Julio celebrates being awarded the "Diamond Disc."

AP/Wide World Photos

Ursula Andress gives Julio a 40th birthday kiss in 1983.
AP/Wide World Photos

Julio and his father meet the press after his father is released from kidnappers. UPI/Bettmann Archive

Julio with his mother, father, brother, sister-in-law, nieces, nephews and his own children.
UPI/Bettmann Archive

Ex-wife Isabel and son Enrique Miguel. UPI/Bettmann Archive

Julio's brother, Carlos.
AP/Wide World Photos

Julio and his three children.
AP/Wide World Photos

Julio and friend at his $3-million home in Biscayne Bay.

Julio at work. AP/Wide World Photos

The face women swoon over. UPI/Bettmann Archive

In concert, an optimistic Julio looks to the future.
AP/Wide World Photos

Much to the singer's shock and disappointment, Isabel refused. Though she had not yet expressed her concerns about his profession, that was high on her list of priorities. Even had that not been the case, as impulsive as Julio has always tended to be, Isabel is just the opposite. She has a logical mind-set reminiscent of Julio's father, and tends to internalize her emotions. The result, Julio says, is that she tends to know "not only what is happening now but also what is going to happen" in the future. Even if something *seems* right, Isabel likes to think about it.

Julio gave her six weeks.

Returning to Madrid after a long stretch on the road, he asked for her hand once again. As millions of concertgoers will attest, Julio can be very persuasive in person, and he gave one of his most sincere performances that night. He spoke to Isabel softly and held her hand, keeping his eyes on her even when she looked away: whenever she'd turn back, there were those deep brown eyes, riveting her.

Uncharacteristically, Isabel let her heart make this decision. Julio was like a pedigree puppy, so adoring and devoted that she not only ignored the warning signs, she agreed to get married at once. One reason is that neither of them wanted to marry "on the fly," and January of 1971 was the only time he knew for certain that he'd be around.

However, a more pressing reason for haste seems to have been a desire to forestall any resistance from their respective families. Today, Julio says discreetly, "The only ones in favor of this marriage were Isabel and I." Whether it was a matter of Isabel's family being suspicious of Julio's mountebank existence, or Julio's parents wondering how he could possibly juggle a family and an all-consuming career, they obviously coun-

seled their children to wait. And, being children, Julio
and Isabel promptly did just the opposite.

He admits now that they behaved impetuously.
"Many times afterward," he reflects, "whenever I thought
this out, I concluded that perhaps it was too short a
time to know each other deep down."

But Julio admits that he wouldn't undo the marriage for anything in the world. He cherishes the love
he and Isabel shared in the early stages of their marriage when, as he puts it, their "youth" came together
and "burned." He also realizes that Isabel did two
things for his career, both of which have been vital to
his present-day success.

The obvious contribution was the way Isabel made
Julio more of a citizen of the world. She came from a
culture considerably different than his own, and in
order to get along with what he calls her "pragmatically
Oriental" nature, he had to temper his "fiery Latin"
one. Nothing frustrated him more than getting into an
argument and raising his voice, only to have her "counter by crawling into the silence of her faraway culture
and philosophy." Though he never quite got the hang of
arguing without shouting, he realized, in time, that to
communicate with any non-Latin—be it Isabel, the
Japanese, the Australians, or, later, the North Americans—
he had to do more than simply master a language. He
had to understand the spirit of the people.

However, what proved to be even more important
to his development as an artist was Isabel's "passive"
interest in his career. Throughout their marriage, nothing would bother him more than the fact that he
couldn't excite his wife about his music. Nothing he
wrote, no concert she attended, no record he cut got
more than her superficial attention. He never understood that, in the beginning, she clearly regarded his

outpourings onstage as childlike and excessive. Coming from a wealthy, aristocratic background, she was accustomed to men who behaved with cool dignity.

Worse, however, is that Julio failed to see, over the years, that she was resenting more and more a career which made him an absentee husband. And therein lies the greatest irony of their marriage.

Because the young couple would brood more than they would communicate, Julio mistakenly believed that he could win her interest by making Isabel proud of him. That suited him just fine, for it meant pushing himself even harder, which he enjoyed. Naturally, these efforts only succeeded in stoking Isabel's resentment. It would take nearly seven years for her emotional boiler to blow and, for all the good that Isabel brought to Julio's life, the last few months of their marriage came perilously close to destroying him.

But hurt and suffering were the farthest things from the young couple's minds on that January 20 morning when they were married. The wedding took place at a church selected by Isabel in neighboring Toledo, after which the lovers honeymooned briefly in the Canary Islands. Then it was back to Madrid, Julio hitting the road to Latin America while Isabel kept busy putting their house in order. Upon learning that their brief honeymoon had left her pregnant, Isabel stayed even busier setting up a nursery.

While the marriage of Julio and Isabel produced its crests and troughs, the high point of the union—indeed, the superlative event in Julio's life—was the birth of his daughter, Chaveli. The significance of the event wasn't entirely apparent in 1971, when burbling Chaveli was simply the new papa's pride and joy, someone to love and coddle while he was relaxing. But as the years passed and she grew more and more like her mother—

eerily so, with Isabel's beauty, composure, and manner-isms—Julio began to see in her the Isabel he had adored when their love was at its peak. That made Chaveli more than just the magical creature any daughter is to her father. She became the personification of a moment in time when all was right with the world, when Julio had all the love he could handle.

Possessing her mother's mien and her father's poetic nature and emotional vulnerability, Chaveli is well-suited to the role of innocent angel. But back in the early 1970s, she was simply Julio's sweet collaborative masterpiece. And to Isabel's chagrin Chaveli was a treasure she was forced to enjoy by herself. The year the girl was born was the same year that Julio went to Belgium, Latin America, Japan, and undertook a Spanish tour in quick succession; as Julio describes it, Isabel saw more of him in the newspapers than she did in the flesh.

Nor was 1972 an improvement. While Julio toured less, he undertook to impress his wife and satisfy his ambition by tackling some formidable professional chores.

He wrote the heartfelt song about his father's homeland, "Canto a Galicia," which became something of an anthem at home and also a breakthrough, number-one recording in North Africa and the Middle East. Galicia is the least Spanish province of Spain and its natives, the gallegos, possess a heritage that is not only Spanish but Celtic and Germanic. Julio captured their melancholy and romantic personality in his song, qualities with which other strongly ethnic peoples identified.

Not only did "Canto a Galicia" bring new audiences into Julio's fold—making it mandatory for him to eventually tour those places—but it ensured his position as one of the preeminent musical artists of the

Spanish-speaking world. After "Life Continues All the Same," it is Julio's favorite song.

Looking to broaden the artist's European base, Columbia had Julio record his first album in German, a record which became a huge hit. It also bred an undercurrent of resentment in Julio, something which plagues him to this day. While it's true that he's sold more records around the world than any singer in history, he has had to do it by rerecording each and every album in the language of the country in which it's to be sold. He complains that he has never had the luxury of a Frank Sinatra or even a Billy Joel: to make an album in his native tongue and have it succeed internationally.

The success of English-language records isn't a virtue of talent, of course, but of the relative universality of English. There are enough English-speaking people to make other versions superfluous. Besides, most artists, English and Spanish alike, simply aren't inclined to learn another language. They're content to be big fish in their respective ponds. Julio is the superambitious exception.

Unfortunately, once Julio finally took the hurdle a decade later and began recording in English, he couldn't simply release those albums around the world. By that time, he had wooed and won the world by singing to each country in its native tongue. To stop now would cause those peoples to feel betrayed, and Julio Iglesias would cease to be an international star. What's worse, he would hurt for having hurt his fans.

His fans. Early in 1973, it started becoming apparent to Isabel that the welfare of his fans was actually more important to Julio than her own. Not overtly, of course. She knew that he loved her, and he was always exceedingly considerate and affectionate when they were with each other. But she began to see that, together,

Julio's fans and his music comprised a lover that was more complex, more versatile, more challenging, more demonstrative, and ultimately more satisfying to him than she could ever hope to be. And that worried her.

But she was already pregnant with their second child, and told herself over and over that maybe this was all temporary, that at some point Julio would reach whatever plateau he was chasing and not have to work so hard.

Had Isabel stuck the marriage out, she'd probably still be waiting.

CHAPTER FIFTEEN

Had Julio been able to reverse the order of events, things would have gone differently on the domestic front. If he'd recorded more and toured less, he would probably still be married. But he had to have an audience before he could have a recording career and, as a result, what had previously been the Julio Express was about to hit a hard and agonizing roadblock.

From 1973 to 1978, Julio spent the bulk of each year on the road. He made all the old tour stops in Europe and Latin America, and was constantly adding new nations to the roster. In 1973 he made his first trip to the U.S., performing to enthusiastic crowds in cities where there was a large Spanish-speaking population. Yet that was just one indication of how popular he was becoming. That same year Julio notched the sale of his ten-millionth album and was awarded an endless array of international honors, among them Venezuela's Guaicaipuro de Oro, Colombia's Antena, Mexico's Heraldo, and Spain's own Pueblo Popular.

The following year, Julio made it onto the Asian charts with *Manuela*, and also launched his first tour of

Canada. He was now recording virtually everything he did in six languages: Spanish, German, Portuguese, Italian, and French, and for the next few years it was imperative not only that he keep the records coming but also that he visit as many countries as possible to keep up his momentum.

By 1979, that kind of frantic schedule would no longer be necessary. Julio would still have a very rigorous year, recording for eight or nine months and spending two or three months on the road. But at least he wouldn't have to do it all simultaneously. He would have time to relax each day before heading to the concert hall or recording studio.

Unfortunately, Isabel didn't wait around for Julio's career to fall into a more regular pattern. Back in 1977, there was just darkness at the end of the tunnel. While she got to travel with him on occasion, Isabel wasn't concerned soley about her own well-being. In addition to Chaveli, Isabel had given birth to young Julio José and baby Enrique, and their father hardly knew them. Whether she and Julio stayed married or separated, they were going to be apart; deciding that anything was better than this marital limbo, she opted for separation.

It was a short, not very sweet, and extremely painful moment when Isabel and Julio agreed that going their separate ways was best. He was in Argentina and, perhaps fittingly, they reached their decision over the telephone.

The conversation was hardly a surprise. The last six months had been sheer hell: whenever they were together, Isabel, behind her shield of resentment, and Julio, with his need to sing, were like two champions locked in battle, refusing to show any mercy or yield an inch of ground. Julio reveals, "The abyss widened between us until our marriage no longer functioned."

His words were understated but his voice moist with sadness when he concluded, "Tragically, our love had left."

The decisive phone conversation between Isabel and Julio was extremely civilized, as was the process which led to their annulment in January of 1979—ironically, on the twentieth of the month, their wedding anniversary. Yet, what followed for Julio was a period of awful, debilitating aftershocks. His mind was plagued by bitter, stinging realizations, any one of which would have thrown him into a rage under ordinary circumstances; under *extraordinary* circumstances, he found them unbearable.

First, Julio had to face the fact that he'd failed at something. And it wasn't something small, like being unable to stop a soccer ball or missing a note during a concert. He'd bungled a marriage and, if that weren't bad enough, everyone who bought his records would soon be reading about it in the newspapers. Never mind whether or not he'd been justified devoting so much time to his career. His family had predicted this confrontation from the start, and he'd chosen to ignore them. He was humiliated and, worse, his confidence was badly eroded. He began to worry that if he'd been wrong about getting married, he could also make serious blunders in his career. And if he couldn't sing, he would die.

Second, while he might have been able to deal with those problems if there had been someone to turn to, the person in whom he'd confided everything for seven years was the one who had just removed herself from his busy life. His family and friends were in Spain and he was on the road; the adoration of his fans was reassuring but faceless. He had always been a loner, but never before had he been truly alone and lonely. It was a numbing experience.

Third, whenever Julio was on the road, he always knew what his children were doing. He'd talk on the phone with them, and Isabel would always fill in the details of whatever Chaveli or the boys had left out. Now it wasn't like that any more. When he spoke with the children, it wasn't with the same ease, laughter, or frequency. The children were upset by the separation, and that only magnified the pain that Julio himself felt.

Finally, because he was dispirited, Julio's work suffered. He was listless and inattentive, utterly unable to put across a song with conviction. Knowing what was happening, yet at the same time being unable to prevent it, made everything that much worse.

"It was a disaster," Julio acknowledges of those months following the agreement to separate. He felt like "a caged animal," and there were nights when he simply couldn't go onstage. "I was broken and anguished," he says, as well as genuinely confused: now that his ardor for Isabel had cooled, he couldn't understand what had possessed him to marry in the first place.

Living from day to day in "a deep depression—constantly and gravely," Julio reached his low point in Caracas. There, his problems blossomed from the purely psychological to the psychosomatic. His legs would go numb and every ounce of strength would drain from his arms. He would touch parts of his body but his fingers wouldn't feel them.

Even in his confused state, Julio recognized that this wasn't like other problems he'd had to face throughout his life, whether it was athletics, overcoming his paralysis, or building a career. This time he was fighting himself, fighting his will to go on being waylaid by guilt and profound sorrow. He felt as though he were "decaying" inside as well as out, and knew that he needed help.

One of the singer's associates in Caracas provided the name of a renowned psychiatrist, and Julio went to see him. For someone as self-sufficient as Julio, confiding in a stranger had to be one of the most difficult things he'd ever done. But once he started talking, the trickle became a flood and he opened up to that doctor in Venezuela as he had to no one before. It was a soul-satisfying confessional, and Julio says that the very patient, very compassionate psychiatrist literally "saved me."

The doctor saw at once that Julio's problem was not only the turmoil in his private life but also the way he seemed to be punishing himself for having married Isabel, for having "made a mistake."

Telling Julio that he wasn't perfect would have been a waste of time, since the singer had trained himself to settle for nothing less. Instead, Julio had to see, first, that his marriage had not been a mistake. The love between him and Isabel may have died, but it *had* been real and it had produced three dearly loved children. It was a relationship that had come to an end, not something that should never have been.

Once the question of failure had been dealt with, Julio had to convince himself that he wasn't bad or reprehensible for having made work his top priority. For one thing, the degree to which he was involved with touring and recording was something neither he nor Isabel could have anticipated seven years before. For another, had he curtailed his efforts to spend nore time at home, he would probably have grown to resent the sacrifice, and that would only have made matters worse. Thus Julio was able to stop flagellating himself for being what he was.

With these two factors put into perspective, it was necessary for Julio to work on the problem of the emotional fallout that was contaminating his work. The doctor helped put Julio back in control by literally scaring him to his senses: the singer was told that until he readjusted to life as a bachelor, his work was all he had. If he destroyed that, he could well destroy himself.

"You have the potential to be your own worst enemy," the doctor concluded. "What you must do is occupy your mind with work so that it can't dwell on anything else."

It's impossible to say what percentage of Julio's recovery was the result of the doctor's "all-work" prescription, and how much was due to the confessional itself. The impact of pouring out his heart cannot be underestimated: it relieved him of his severest pressures and allowed him to breathe again.

Regardless, after the visit Julio began to function more normally. His physical maladies vanished, and though Isabel and the children were frequently on his mind, he was able to channel the emotional energy he was feeling into creative productivity.

"It became my refuge," he says, "my life became a thing of authentic masochism." If he weren't performing or recording, he was inevitably en route to do so— "today in Istanbul," he says, "tomorrow in Zamora." When he was alone he spent his time writing or, if what he was feeling was too strong to put on paper, he busied himself with language studies, perfecting familiar tongues. He had not yet recorded in English, and he made that one of his top priorities; but since it was such a critical market, he didn't want to approach it half-cocked. So he studied for hours on end, sometimes with tapes and books, at other times with a tutor. Like the doctor had recommended, Julio didn't give himself an instant to dwell on his sorrow.

The road back to stability wasn't easy, but Julio was profoundly relieved to discover that it would at least be navigable. And today, with the benefit of both maturity and hindsight, he has come to believe that the marriage was, in fact, a good thing. Not only did it give him his beloved children but, in its early days, it gave him the opportunity to love a woman fervently. That has never again happened to the same degree and, countless lovers later, whenever Julio is asked by an interviewer to name the first woman that comes to mind, it is always Isabel.

"The love has left completely," he insists with a trace of regret. "That flame is gone." But he is quick to add that there are no ashes. "Only the glitter remains," he says, smiling, "the memories, full of colors good and bad but above all *human.*"

If the Julio who came through the crucible of marriage was not quite the superhuman he'd been before, he was without question a better "human." While that didn't stop him from setting outrageous goals for himself—most of which he would attain, as it happens—his unique blend of audacity and determination was tempered with humility.

An example of just *how* well-adjusted the new Julio was to become raised a few eyebrows in Spain during the closing months of 1984. Four years earlier Isabel had remarried, tying the knot with a nobleman, the cheerful if plain-looking Carlos Falco, Marquis of Griñon. A year later she bore him a daughter, Tamara—a girl who, like Chaveli, has her mother's looks and mannerisms and her father's disposition.

When Tamara was three, Isabel decided that for the first time in her thirty-two years she would like to

go out and earn a wage. The profession she selected
was journalism, writing for the *Life*-like magazine *¡Hola!*,
and the subject she chose for her first interview was
Julio. She made her request through channels and,
with equal pluck, Julio agreed to see her.

The ex-husband and wife had been together on
family occasions such as birthdays and holidays, but this
was the first time they'd been by themselves since he
left for the fateful trip to Argentina. Upon her arrival at
Julio's estate in Indain Creek, Florida, there were
embraces and smiles for the *¡Hola!* photographers, and
pictures of the ex-lovers at ease with their children.
Then the photgraphers left and one of the most unlikely
interviews of all time got under way.

Isabel was the picture of efficiency: she had her
questions written neatly on a legal pad, had two cassette recorders running in case one malfunctioned, and
even dressed for the occasion, wearing a drab but
businesslike brown dress.

She asked her questions with professional detach-
ment, inquiring about his newfound success in the
U.S., his lifestyle in Florida, his fans and future plans,
and even about his family. Dressed casually in white
trousers and a plain white T-shirt, with a navy blue
windbreaker slung over his shoulders, Julio was equally
forthright in his answers; Isabel later commented that
he "answered everything I asked" without hedging or
discomfort.

Like most other interviewers, Isabel only got a half
hour of her husband's very valuable time. It was a
professional meeting, top to bottom. But the ease with
which they communicated, and the mutual admiration
each demonstrated for the other, showed just how far
they had come in five years.

Shortly thereafter, rumors of a rift between the

marquis and his bride began to surface in the Spanish press. Though Julio insists he will never again marry, what may happen in the future is anyone's guess. After all, who would have thought, back in 1978, that in just a few short years those two bitter antagonists would be kissing and smiling for the cameras. . . .

Chapter Sixteen

A French newspaper once took a long, hard look at the career of Julio Iglesias, and decided that there were seven reasons to explain his phenomenal success.

In no particular order, they are:
1 He's elegant onstage,
2 He's handsome and trim,
3 He has a good smile,
4 He makes women believe every word he sings,
5 He maintains his classy look offstage,
6 He sings hits from all the musical modes and eras, and
7 He sings about love and pain and makes women want to comfort him.

All of these qualities came naturally, though some required a bit more refinement than the others. This is especially true of the last entry. Julio was a great balladeer from the start, but only after wading through the shambles of his marriage did he learn enough about pain and women to make his fans want to protect and ravage him simultaneously.

He spent six months learning to cope with the pain; now it was time for him to find out more about women.

Although Julio immersed himself in his career, he actually accomplished little more than to gild the professional lily. The momentum he had built up continued to carry him higher, and he was soon one of the top-selling recording artists in the world.

In that disastrous year of 1977, a concert in the national stadium of Santiago, Chile—home of that first, small fan club of his—was attended by over one hundred thousand swooning fans. His album *El Amor* became the best-selling record not only in Spain but in most of continental Europe, Latin America, Canada, the Middle East, and in various African nations. That feat was matched the following year by the album *33 Años*; 1978 was also the year in which he released his first Italian and French albums—*Sono un Pirata, Sono un Signore* and *Aimer la Vie,* respectively—both of which became number-one hits. To no one's surprise, the recording industries of France, Italy, Germany, and other countries unanimously chose Julio as their "Artist of the Year."

Concurrent with breaking musical records one after the other, Julio was also being honored outside the industry. Countless clothing societies named him to their "Ten Best-Dressed Men" lists, and as far back as 1976 the press was already referring to him as the "New Valentino."

Julio admits to knowing next to nothing about Mr. Valentino, save that he was a romantic silent-film star. But he warrants that after he put his marriage behind him, he did indeed become an "expert" on the subject of women.

"I am not being presumptuous," he says candidly, "but it is my *job* to know about women. Which doesn't mean I would ever take advantage of a woman. I would shoot myself before I would do something like that. Rather, I *feel* with them . . . I understand their needs."

Having been out of circulation for seven years, Julio spent a lot of time boning up on the gaps in his knowledge of "feeling" with women. And in short order the Valentino label became something of a self-fulfilling prophecy as, step-by-step, lover by lover, Julio's private life took on the intense romanticism of his stage persona—with one important difference.

Onstage, Julio gives his heart freely. He can afford to: flirting with women in the audience is a brief, impersonal offering. Which is not to say that it's affected; it isn't. He's genuinely moved by these people, from the nun who left the convent after hearing him sing, to the man who brought his crippled daughter to see Julio in the hope that he could cure her. He wants to make their fantasy real for just an hour.

Offstage, however, he is more cautious. Before he commits to a woman, even for a night, he likes to feel that it's *him* she wants, "with my weak legs" and scarred back, and not just Julio Iglesias the singer.

In all fairness to Julio, he has reason to be suspicious. He's constantly finding gifts and marriage proposals among the five hundred-plus fan letters which reach him every day; nor are they all he receives from his admirers.

One night, Julio returned to a hotel room and, undressing quickly—Julio usually sleeps in the nude—he fell into bed. "All of a sudden," he remembers, "I felt something on my back, something which ran up and down my spine."

Turning on the light and examining the mattress, he found nothing there and went back to sleep. However, almost at once he felt an insistent stab and, fearful that his old pain was returning, he shouted for his friend and manager, Alfredo Fraile, who was in a room nearby.

Alfredo came rushing in and, noticing a leg sticking from the other side of the bed, pulled on it and found it attached to a fully clothed young lady.

Weeping, the woman explained to the startled singer that she'd hidden herself under the bed in order to meet him, but had become frozen with fear when he finally arrived. She had been moving in a feeble effort to get out unnoticed—hence the stabbing at Julio's back.

Her clothes wrinkled and her hair disheveled, the poor woman was escorted from the room by Alfredo. However, just before she disappeared into the hallway, she paused and turned to her exhausted and frankly unnerved host. "Forgive me, Julio!" she cried plaintively. "I only wanted to sleep with you!"

As a result of that incident Julio makes a point of looking under the bed whenever he enters a hotel room—especially if he's already *with* a woman. And while it may be difficult to feel sorry for Julio, it's clear that he genuinely craves love in his sexual relationships. And when he finds it, even if only for a night, he treats that paramour like a queen.

Women who fall into that category tend to know who they are. If Julio likes them, he not only spends the night with them but, if he has no other obligations, stays in bed with them through the following morning and into the next night. "I'm not the type of man who leaves a woman after making love," he says in obvious understatement, "nor do I turn around and fall asleep immediately."

With Julio, while the "erotic" aspects of lovemaking are vitally important, he puts equal value on the "feelings" of love. And while he has no use for exotic trappings, be they mirrored ceilings or satin sheets, he does place a high value on sexual creativity.

"I am an extremely creative person when it comes to lovemaking," he reveals. "Imagination is fundamental. My body needs to be made love to every day and every night, [and] it must be done in an imaginative form. Somewhat revoluntionary, but biologically correct."

To this end, Julio insists on having no interest whatsoever in homosexuality. He seems particularly sensitive when discussing the matter because of his mantle as the New Valentino—Valentino reportedly having been fond of both sexes.

"I understand homosexuals," Julio says, weighing his words carefully, "and I do not criticize them. I have them near me; they're wonderful creators, sometimes the best. But I'm not going to go in that direction. It isn't within me."

Patronizing prostitutes is also something which has never appealed to him. Yet, while he has never "paid for love," he comes across as being more empathetic to their lifestyle than to that of gays, referring to them with rather poetic euphemisms, such as "those who never see the sun," "women without a name," and "those who sell love."

Whether or not there is a hidden value judgment in his detached observations about gays and his romanticized view of prostitutes only Julio can say.

After playing the field for several years, Julio found

that as a "type" he was particularly attracted to airline stewardesses. He says that they tend to be cheerful, pretty, and ready to please. He also loves them, he says, because he associates them with the satisfying sense of speed and freedom he derives from airplanes. Apart from that, he doesn't respond to any special type, background, nationality, or physical "aesthetic." He absolutely insists on "intelligence and tenderness" in a lover, and prefers women who don't wear perfume. "The odor of love," he says, "is the odor that I love. The natural one. The only one, no matter how animalistic it is."

Other than that, he's wide open. Skin color is singularly unimportant to him. Says Julio, "It doesn't matter whether it's very white, very dark, the color of cane, or golden. I simply like skin."

The public record bears out Julio's eclectic tastes. One day he might be entertaining a Puerto Rican model at Indian Creek; the next day a stewardess with Air France might pop in for a visit. On the road, he may find himself sharing "unforgettable memories" with a reigning Miss Universe in Australia, or else might be out on the town with one of the numerous celebrities to whom he's been linked since he and Isabel parted.

As it turns out, celebrities have been his most regular companions, accrued as a result of Julio's rising fame during the late 1970s. Yet, while he's been seen with the likes of Bianca Jagger, Ursula Andress, stunning Polynesian actress Vaitiare Hirschon, and even Brooke Shields ("She has one of the most beautiful faces in the world," he enthuses), he has only been really close to a pair of stars.

The dearest of his celebrity girlfriends has always been actress Sydne Rome. Relatively unknown in the U.S., the thirty-eight-year-old actress was born in Akron,

Ohio, and made her fame as a star of Spanish and Italian films. Blond and blue-eyed, she is far from an acting heavyweight. But as a screen beauty, she is second to none.

Julio first saw her on the screen early in the 1970s. He had always found her attractive and, when he and Isabel parted, he expressed a desire to meet her. The opportunity arose late in 1979, when Julio was in Italy. They had both been invited to a dinner and, upon arriving, Julio says he conspired "to do everything I could to sit next to her." Looking into her "beautiful eyes," he was mesmerized; he became even more enraptured after some hours had passed and she revealed herself to have the great style of an Italian but the supple mind of an American, a "formidable cocktail." Sydne obviously felt a similar attraction, and the seed of their romance was planted.

The fact that Sydne was married was a bother, but not enough to stop love from taking its course. "Her marriage was not working," Julio says defensively. "Everyone knew it; I was not responsible for it."

Though their work took them to different corners of the world—rarely at the same time—they did manage to rendezvous as often as possible for the duration of their romance. "It wasn't easy," Julio recalls, "but whenever we could, we did." Once, Sydne, who is Jewish, even journeyed to Beirut at the height of Lebanese-Israeli tensions just to be with her lover.

Eventually, however, the lovers went their separate ways. Not only were they separated by distance, but Julio was inevitably working when Sydne was not, and that made getting together difficult. "Again," he laments, he was dealt a cruel hand by "the damn holy destiny that unites everything and breaks up everything. The compromise, the kilometers—perhaps they killed a most formidable story of love."

Yet, while Sydne and Julio are rarely in touch, they still think fondly of one another, and the singer hints that the door is open for a resumption of their passion at some future date.

In any case, Sydne is always around him in the form of Julio's beloved pointer, Hey, so named after one of the singer's most successful albums. Though Julio has two other dogs—the German Shepherds Max and Guapa—the black-and-white Hey is the canine light of his life. Sydne gave him the dog in Europe, and not only is it his most trusted companion—the dog sleeps on Julio's right-hand pillow when no woman is present—but Hey was the first dog to have a seat on the Concorde. The captain, and presumably the other passengers, were less than delighted to be sharing a compartment with Julio's pup. However, by that time Julio had the clout to get what he wanted, and what he wanted was for Hey to be at his side.

The other star who became an intimate of Julio's was Elvis Presley's former wife Priscilla. They met when she did a TV special with him, and he was "fascinated" by her. Apart from her beauty and wit, he was impressed by the fact that she refused to capitalize on the reputation of Elvis. She was strong, individualistic, and committed to personal excellence. What's more, she liked many of the things which were important to Julio: travel, dancing, animals, and being in the fresh air. And she was also a romantic, sending flowers for no particular reason and writing letters from wherever she was—which, on one occasion, included Japan, where she happened to meet Sydne Rome. Julio does not know if they compared notes.

Alas, once again, distance proved to be Julio's

undoing. It was impossible for them to be together enough to nurture a relationship. Thus, while their affection didn't die, neither did it flourish.

If ever a fan, friend, or journalist needed to know just *how* important singing is to Julio, the list of romantic casualties is as graphic a yardstick as one could ask for. Gwendoline, Isabel, Sydne, and Priscilla: other artists may have suffered more than Julio for their art, but few have suffered as deeply.

Yet, with all the comings and goings of women in Julio's world, the steady lovers and one-night stands who have taught him much of what there is to know about women, there *is* one constant in the singer's love life: a sense of resilience and optimism. Asked when he last slept with a woman, Julio always rhapsodizes, "Tomorrow." In that short but bittersweet reply, Julio almost seems to be yearning for a princess, someone to turn the knight from dragon-slaying to castle-building.

Whether that can be achieved by *any* mortal woman remains to be seen. In the meantime, as even Julio concedes, he's having a not-terribly-painful time finding out.

CHAPTER SEVENTEEN

While Julio was having his ups and downs romantically, he had no trouble whatsoever on the professional front. By 1979 he was among the five top-selling recording artists in the world; by 1983 he would reach the number-one spot, an achievement *The Guinness Book of World Records* commemorated by awarding the world's only diamond record.

Things had really begun to snowball for the singer the year his marriage was annulled. The pivotal year of 1979 saw the release of the album *Emociónes*, which overshadowed the sales of Julio's previous records and sparked his most comprehensive and successful world tour to date. Nor did the momentum slow the following year: in 1980 his album *Hey* overtook the all-time high set by *Emociónes*, becoming the biggest-selling album in no less than eighty countries around the world. Women of all ages loved him, men didn't find him threatening, the poor and rich alike claimed him as one of their own; his was proving to be a truly universal appeal.

What's more, he cut across all political barriers.

Fidel Castro made it known he was a fan, as did the late General Omar Torrijos of Panama, whom Julio once described as "a splendid personality." One day he was being honored by General Anastasio Somoza of Nicaragua, the next day by the majordomos of the Sandinistas. Nancy Reagan went to hear him sing (and later had him over to the White House), Princess Grace asked him to perform in Monaco (where, after seeing her close up for the first time, he found himself absolutely enchanted by her smile), and Egyptian President Anwar Sadat became a fast friend after the singer performed in Egypt (where he also met one of the president's six daughters, with whom he became an item). Needless to say, King Juan Carlos of Spain is a great admirer of his nation's most important export, and Julio is one of the monarch's biggest and most vocal boosters.

In fact, the only part of the world where he has always been greeted with a noticeable lack of enthusiasm is, incredibly, Galicia. Because Julio's ancestors hail from that part of the country, the natives have expected him to behave like one of them. But his accent and pronunciation are different, and he has fallen far short of being the cultural ambassador they had hoped he would be. Their attitude hurts Julio, and he admits that even today he dwells upon it a great deal. But he has also come to realize that he can't be all things to all people, and fears that if he were to change and become a proselyte, he would disappoint more people than he would please.

With the ongoing exception of Galicia, Julio enjoyed unparalleled professional triumphs during 1979–1980, and they were a balm which began to lift him from his depression. That, in turn, helped get him into the swing of going out with women again, which completed his recovery, and also made him even more newsworthy.

It's axiomatic that the bigger any star becomes, the more they become targets of the press. Julio was no exception. His liaisons with some of the world's most famous and lovely women made him a popular subject for exploitation, while he also became the whipping boy of critics and journalists who were looking to make a name for themselves by trashing a superstar.

Of the two, the personal stories have been the most intrusive and the most annoying. What bothers him most is that they don't only involve him, they involve his family as well as his lovers. And since Julio doesn't talk a lot about his personal life, much of the information is obtained secondhand or on the fly. Julio has had to deal with reporters who've disguised themselves as security guards at concerts in order to eavesdrop and pick up snippets of information and, on one occasion, he was even engaged in conversation by a little old lady who, he later learned, had been wired for sound.

By Julio's reckoning, more than half of the material in the fifteen thousand-plus articles which have been published about his life is untrue—not surprising, given the way it's obtained. That's one of the reasons Julio makes himself as available as possible to the press. Individual reporters—his ex-wife included—may not enjoy a lot of time with the singer, but at least the information they get is all firsthand.

Which is not to say that it's therefore accurate. On occasion, Julio *will* skew an interview to create a particular impression. For example, when he was interviewed by the upscale *Architectural Digest* in 1984, Julio took pains to discuss the Spanish Republican poet Antonio Machado, the impressionistic Spanish

novelist Pío Baroja, and the Colombian novelist Gabriel
García Márques. In fact, Julio detests reading with a
passion. He hardly ever reads, and when he does, his
preferred subject matter is celebrity biographies and
autobiographies. His familiarity with Ernest Hemingway
seems to extend little farther than the fact that he was
model Margaux Hemingway's grandfather. But he obviously wanted to create an aura of wide-ranging
literacy for the audience of *Architectural Digest*. He
happened to be under fire at the time for having
embraced the United States at the expense of his
Latin fans. Openly and proudly lauding those three
important Spanish-language writers helped to defuse
some of the criticism.

For whatever reason he's giving an interview, Julio
finds the process itself almost as painful as reading
misinformation. "It's not easy to put one's life on dis-
play for the world," he acknowledges, but it's more
difficult still "to go backward" for an interview, "to
relive the past. Sometimes they're open wounds or
poorly healed scars and when you pick on them the pus
that comes out has a terrible odor." In order to make
the job easier, he frequently reminds himself that his
mother's father was a journalist, and that one of these
reporters may be using the money they earn to buy
their own little Julio a soccer ball. His sentimentality
may be one of the qualities that makes Julio wound so
easily—he is one of the quickest criers he knows—but
it's also his lifeline to humanity in an industry not noted
for its sensitivity.

Yet, even having made these sacrifices, it's the lot
of any artist to suffer not only the scrutiny of the
gossip columnists but also the whims and moods of the
critics. And while Julio has been more fortunate than

most performers, he has come in for his share of criticism.

Most of the negative comments he received prior to 1983 were directed at the disproportionate, and certainly unexpected, size of his following in relation to his talent and artistic innovation. Elvis and the Beatles were popular, but they'd changed the face of music; Julio did nothing of the kind. Typical of the mystified reviewers was Latin music critic Agustín Gurza, who marveled that a "prolonged standing ovation" Julio received "seemed well out of proportion with the actual substance of his performance," while the show-business journal *Variety* noted of his first appearance at Madison Square Garden that nonfans would most likely find his "laidback, non-energetic show boring." *Variety* was even more critical at a later date, when they found his performance "formulaic . . . slushy [and] lacking in timbral excitement."

However, if there has been one recurrent criticism of Julio Iglesias, it's been that his act is pure "shtick": affected mannerisms and artless routines calculated to achieve a certain result. That result, according to his critics, is to have women sighing and moaning each time Julio's velvet tenor cracks or snags with emotion.

Julio himself is deeply hurt by this impression. "It has been said about me, in effect, that I say, 'I love you, I love you, I *worship* you' in a loud voice. And then, in a much lower voice, I whisper, 'and I charge you for it.'" He swears that there isn't enough money in the world to make him say he loves anyone if he doesn't genuinely feel it.

While it's true that Julio's manner has become more *polished* with time, and to a degree predictable— he has, after all, given over 2,200 live concerts and taped nearly 900 TV shows—he is justified at being indignant. Julio Iglesias may be smooth, but he is neither insincere nor aloof.

On one level, he is constantly challenged and charged not only by the different audiences he sees but also by the contrasting locales he visits—celebrated nightclubs and auditoriums from Monte Carlo to Carnegie Hall to the most historic spots on earth, including the pyramids in Egypt and the Roman Colosseum. That kind of thrill, he insists, keeps his creative energies at a peak.

On another, much deeper level, of course, there are the fans. Their enthusiasm is contagious, and when they respond to him, he responds to them. The result is electricity and synergy which is anything but contrived. To an outsider, this communication may seem like nothing more than Julio smiling boyishly as a sea of women throw flowers at the stage while swooning and calling for him to take their hearts, their bodies, or both. But to Julio and his fans, that's just the outward manifestation of a very real rapport. Julio goes out of his way to strengthen this bond by changing the words of his songs, something which *personalizes* a performance and gives it greater intimacy.

As Julio has said, he does not take this affection lightly. Whenever he learns that he has even indirectly disappointed a fan—whether it was because they didn't have the money to buy a concert ticket, or they walked one hundred kilometers only to arrive too late to see him get onto an airplane (as one girl did in Chile) —Julio will call that person to thank them and to make arrangements to see them at some future date. That's more than simple rapport: that's love and, as Julio has said, he genuinely loves his fans as deeply as they love him.

* * *

Because of the power and responsibility Julio wields when he goes forth to meet his fans, it's interesting to note that, for the singer, the very act of preparing for the stage is very solemn, something which borders on being a religious experience. The proof of this is in the ritualistic, almost monastic way Julio prepares for each show.

He arrives at a site two or three hours before the concert is to begin. There, he personally checks the sound from all points of the hall, to make sure that everyone will be able to hear him clearly. If only a few people have arrived, he'll usually go over and greet them, their faces helping to juice him up for the performance.

Retiring to his dressing room, he'll eat nothing but sip several cups of hot tea with honey, which helps to loosen up his voice. If at all possible, Julio tries to spend this time alone, except for his assistant-cum-valet— at present, a sixty-year-old woman named Jennie. (Julio cracks that many women *undress* him, but she is the only woman who *dresses* him.)

Although isolation isn't always possible with fans, reporters, business associates, photographers, family members, and friends all vying for a piece of his time, Julio finds that a few minutes alone in a "zone of silence" produces the best results onstage. In this way, the singer is not unlike stage actors, most of whom require a half hour or so before a show in order to get into character.

Even if there are people present, Julio does not digress from his "special ceremony," the one which insures his head-to-toe dignity and elegance. Stripping, he showers and then puts on his shirt, which must be long-sleeved, the color of ivory, and have buttons rather than cuff links. The snug fit at the wrists derives from his sense of style; the long sleeves are important because he usually removes his jacket and tosses it into the audience.

As for the off-white color, that's the most important to Julio personally. It's a reminder of that long-ago trip to Viña del Mar, when he sang in his second festival. His shirt had been lost by the hotel cleaner and, with nothing else to wear, Julio had had to borrow a dirty shirt from another performer. Even though he was an unknown dressed in another man's shirt, Chile embraced him; wearing a "dirty" shirt today is his way of remembering how important his fans are to his success and well-being.

After the shirt is buttoned—always top to bottom, so it will settle smoothly over his broad shoulders—he snuggles into his black silk underpants. Julio makes it a habit never to wear white underwear: it wouldn't do for the bright lights of the stage to render them visible beneath his trousers.

The navy blue pants are next, cut so they'll hang exactly two centimeters above his shoes and tailored so that they can be worn beltless, "like a second skin." Each pair is also meticulously double-stitched around the zipper. In Paris once, performing at the Olympia, Julio had to continue singing after his fly had burst—a "dramatic" situation he does not care to repeat.

However, that isn't the only unusual aspect to the trousers. If Julio has used a paper napkin at any time during the day, he places that napkin in his pocket and keeps it with him for the rest of the day. "I don't know whether it's a psychiatric problem or kleptomania," says Julio, but it's one of his only superstitions (the other big one is refusing to wear yellow onstage, reportedly because he was wearing that color the night of the accident), and he refuses to explore or discontinue the habit. If nothing else, it comes in handy if he becomes tense or nervous. At such times, he'll remove it, roll it pencil thin, and tickle his ear with it.

Without tucking in his shirt, Julio then attends to his hair. Apart from his tan, about which he is a fanatic—Julio tries to avoid performing in any part of the world where he won't be able to get his daily ration of sun—he is most self-conscious about his hair. Not that every strand has to be in place; indeed, if it becomes untidy during an emotional moment, so much the better. Julio is a moderately vain man, but not a plastic one. Rather, the singer is concerned that his coiffure cover any hints of baldness. Julio's father has lost most of his hair in the front, and Julio's own hairline has proven far from immutable. Since he vows never to wear a toupee, Julio takes extra care to sculpt his hair evenly and securely across his forehead.

Next, Julio dons his slim-knotted silk tie and then his vest. The vest must be even tighter than his pants, so tight that it "hurts," he says, "even to the point of constricting me." This isn't another example of the singer punishing himself, but simply a concession to the fact that he'll be standing for well over an hour. His back has never been as strong as it was before the operation, and Julio says that a tight vest helps hold him up onstage. It also helps him sing. Though Julio says that the words "come from my heart, the volume comes from my stomach," and the vest helps squeeze it out.

With the vest in place, Julio proceeds to tuck in his shirttails. Following that, he slips on his shoes, which have been specially made with thin soles. That allows him to feel the music vibrating under his feet and to stay loose. What's more, if he's about to put on a pair of shoes he hasn't worn before, they've already been artifically broken in. Since Julio has always spent a great deal of his leisure time barefoot or wearing loose-fitting tennis shoes (even though he has no interest in tennis), he can't possibly be at ease onstage unless his feet are comfortable.

After checking himself in the mirror, Julio pulls on his seven hundred dollar jacket and leaves the dressing room in silence. Right before he goes on, he will stand in the wings and scream several times; sharp-eared concertgoers can usually hear him. He does this to relax, since the last three or four minutes before he goes on are particularly nerve-wracking. Not so coincidentally, three minutes is exactly how long it took him to muster the courage to go onstage at Benidorm.

Then, the instant before he goes on, he usually stares at the palms of his hands. He will have washed them several times in his dressing room—no one knows why, not even Julio. Doubtless it has to do with the importance his hands play in each performance, one holding the microphone, the other constantly moving through the air, reaching for his heart, or accepting a hand or rose extended to him from the first row.

This ritual is no different whether Julio is performing in a dusty stadium in South America or in an elegant concert hall in London. It helps him to put aside the private Julio Iglesias, that relatively introspective man, and bring out the poised, outgoing singer the fans have come to see, hear, and touch.

The entire process is a possession, in a way, a supplanting of one spirit by another. In fact, when it's over, he goes through the equivalent of an exorcism.

Leaving the stage, his tight clothes damp with sweat, he allows no one to touch him save for his valet. When they're alone, he'll peel off his damp clothing, fall into a plush blue robe, and sit quietly as Jennie, or whomever, massages his feet with lotion. During a performance, Julio says, "I'll press my toes against the floor," his one concession to nerves. Afterward, *he* can't relax until *they're* relaxed.

But that's not all he does while he's lying there. He and his valet are silent so that Julio can listen to the musicians as they leave the stage. They invariably discuss the show, and he likes to hear what they have to say. Apart from the brutally candid comments his father makes ("If he doesn't like it, he has no problem telling me," Julio says, laughing), the singer says that the musicians are just about the best critics he has.

All of which adds up to what is admittedly a very eccentric process for Julio. But, contrary to what many of his critics imply, it clearly isn't a *phony* process, by any means. Julio likens it to the preparations of a boxer or an ancient gladiator before entering the arena, and the analogy is a fair one. Like a fighter, he must be sensitive to every move and shift his opponent makes— in this case, his "adversary" being the expectations of the audience. It's one of the oddest paradoxes of his career that after all of Julio's formal preparations in the dressing room, the shows themselves percolate with spontaneity.

However, stage performances have only been a part of the Julio Iglesias success story. Before the concert comes the record, which Julio approaches with even greater dedication and intensity. He equates his fans with the thief who once stole Da Vinci's "Mona Lisa" from the Louvre. He didn't take the painting to sell it, but simply to enjoy it in his home. Without making a qualitative judgment or intending to sound pompous, Julio says that his fans approach his albums with the same kind of reverence.

For that reason, Julio insists that "the record must be full of magic. I'm obsessed with that, with carrying a record from another world, where it is born, to this world," with the magic intact.

Concerts are begun and ended within two hours. The albums, however, are quite another matter.

CHAPTER EIGHTEEN

J ust as 1979 was a turning point in so many ways, it was also the year Julio started touring less and recording more. It wasn't so much a matter of choice but of necessity. While Julio's Spanish-language albums still outsold the nearest runner-up, the French albums, by a four-to-one margin, he gave them equal attention when they were recorded, just as he did his albums in German, Italian, and Portuguese.

All of this was very time-consuming, and in order to keep up with the demand for fresh material in each language, Julio had no choice but to spend more time in the studio. Often, to give him a breather (read: time to tour), CBS would put together special "packages" for each market—tunes in other languages which were new to the Julio-hungry countries. But the Portuguese "*Abracame*" didn't play quite as well in Germany as "*Wo Bist Du,*" so new material had to be generated on a regular basis.

By this time, Julio was no longer recording in London, but was dividing his time between a facility in the Bahamas, the CBS studios in New York, and the Criteria Studios in Miami. He particularly liked record-

ing in Miami because the city was centrally located
relative to the many points in the world he frequently
had to visit, especially Central and South America and
Europe.

Miami also appealed to Julio because of its tropical
climate and perpetual sunshine, and for an even more
important reason: it was located in the United States.

Though he barely had time to sleep given his
present workload, Julio was beginning to wonder if it
might not be possible to make a successful assault on
the English-language market. No Spanish artist had
ever succeeded to any significant degree, and for the
world's most popular recording artist the temptation
was too sweet to ignore.

But the time wasn't right, he knew. For one thing,
his English wasn't good enough. For another, he hadn't
spent a lot of time with Americans and knew very little
about American sensibilities, an understanding which
would be necessary if he were to effectively sing to and
communicate with American women. Finally, it was
not a project to be undertaken without a hefty war
chest and several years of meticulous groundwork.

However, he had realized that he could at least
begin a lot of this homework if he were living in Miami,
and he built a house there in 1978. In the meantime,
however, he had some records to cut, and those required his fullest attention.

Wherever Julio records, his producer and very
close friend Ramón Arcusa is always at his side. Ramón
and Manuel de la Calva once comprised the popular
Spanish singing group Duo Dinamico, a team which
disbanded, says Arcusa, when the Beatles came along
and made them feel "that our music was too old." Julio
had first met him at Viña del Mar and says, "He is, I
think, the person with whom I spend the most time in

my life." With the exception of his Benidorm companion, Singer Manolo Otero, Julio says that Ramón "was my earliest friend and teacher in music."

Four years older than Julio, the tall, rangy Ramón is also Julio's professional anchor. Just as Chaveli gives Julio's personal life value however low he feels, Ramón sees Julio through every professional blow. "He is my advisor, a little bit my older brother, and on many nights my sympathizer," admits Julio. "I owe one hundred percent of what I have to him."

Throughout the eight or nine months that Julio and Ramón spend in the studio—including Saturdays and Sundays—their routine is invariably the same. Having spent the night before in the studio, Julio will wake around eleven o'clock, doing leg exercises by his pool and having some breakfast before Ramón arrives shortly after noon. Wherever they are, the men will go outside and review the music they'll be taping that night. If there's something that doesn't sit well with Julio or Ramón, they'll mark it and, when they've run through all the music at least once, retire to the nearest piano.

This fine-tuning of a piece can last anywhere from an hour to an entire afternoon, and during that period Julio will see or talk to no one else. It is an often heated period of creativity, particularly if Julio and Ramón don't see eye-to-eye on something. In the science of music and engineering, Ramón is Julio's superior; in terms of commercial instinct—sensing the impact of the instruments, words, or progressions—Julio has the edge. The two worlds don't always mesh, and at those times it requires an inordinate amount of patience on the producer's part to reach some kind of compromise. Julio tends to get very emotional and stubborn where music is concerned, and Ramón ("God bless him," Julio notes) is the one who has to bend over backward to keep the collaboration from becoming, in Julio's words, "an explosive" one.

Regardless of what hour they finish, Julio remains in the sun until it's time to tape. This isn't only the result of his vanity; Julio finds recording studios to be stuffy, "Byzantine crypts" which become inordinately depressing if he hasn't had his daily dose of fresh air. Outside, seated beside a phone, he will conduct business, give interviews, or simply visit with his children, parents, or friends.

Naturally, if it has been raining, Julio finds it difficult to muster his energies for music or for anything else. Rain, he complains, "fills me with sadness that saturates my soul," and though that offers creative dividends in the studio, just getting there requires a Herculean effort.

Rain or shine, it is always early evening before Julio heads to the studio. He likes to drive himself rather than to be taken by a chauffeur. That way, he doesn't sit and brood and become anxious about what he has to do. Like many artists, Julio is instinctively drawn to the negative and seems to feel that if he stops to analyze his talent or dwell upon it at length, either his voice will up and leave him or he'll simply forget the musical sense he's acquired.

This notion that his abilities may be a myth or a dream is actually a common fear among overachievers. Speaking for most successful artists, Paul McCartney said it best: "They can think I'm as famous as they like, but in back of it all there's always this sneaking feeling it's not really true." Like many of his peers, McCartney honestly fears that he's going to wake up one day and find himself "bumming around on some beach looking for a meal."

Julio's innate negativism about himself is one of the

reasons he's fanatic about surrounding himself with upbeat, patient people like Ramón. Sourpusses are quickly pink-slipped, and while Julio admits "That may sound cruel," he insists that it would be crueler by far to disappoint fans by allowing himself to become glum and downbeat.

A mundane activity like driving helps prevent Julio from becoming too reflective. En route he often chews gum to relax, and if his current lover, the mysterious "La Flaca," is in for a visit, she will probably have prechewed it before he goes.

No doubt Julio is comforted to be taking a part of his lover to work, since he almost never permits anyone who is not involved in the creation of a record to enter the studio. For one thing, it's distracting. The only person he wants to have on his mind is that fan who will be listening to his album, listening as though the recording were their "Mona Lisa." For another, so many of the sessions produce work that is beneath his standards, and he simply doesn't want anyone else to hear it. He says it would be unutterably detrimental to his work if he were to look over to the booth and see disappointment in the face of a friend or fan.

When Julio records, the only musicians that are present are a small rhythm section, usually a bass guitar and a piano. The orchestra and backup singers are recorded later, under Ramón's supervision, though the actual overlaying of the tracks is overseen by Ramón and Julio both.

Thus, every night of those months-long stretches, he sits alone in the studio, just like he did during that first session for Columbia. The people in the booth—Ramón, a handful of engineers, and a language tutor who double-checks his work in tongues other than Spanish—are disembodied voices who communicate with

Julio and his patient rhythm musicians through ear-
phones. Every hour or so they'll take a break, Julio and
Ramón usually heading to a vending machine for a
candy bar or to the refrigerator for a paper cupful of
orange juice. While they stand there, the men don't
relax: either they'll review the next piece of music or, if
something isn't right, they'll huddle to discuss the
problem until they find a solution. And if they go back
to the session and discover that something *still* isn't
working, be it the music, the arrangement, or Julio's
delivery, they'll keep at it until it comes together, which
is often in the very small hours of the morning.

"Those sessions tire me," Julio says, "and sometimes deteriorate my nerves." But his reverence for the
finished product won't allow him to give up. He regards
each record as a "vehicle [which] carries me rapidly
around the world." He would no sooner send it out
flawed than he would appear onstage in shirt-sleeves.
Even if the problem is a very minor one, a nuance only
he and Ramón will pick up in the finished product, it
must be fixed. Julio firmly believes that if he were to
compromise his personal standards even once, no matter how small the infraction, the domino effect would
be disastrous. Before long he would get sloppy in other
areas, and he simply couldn't face himself or his fans if
he failed to give them the quality they expect and
deserve.

Aside from the impact a bad album would have on
his career, Julio has been a perfectionist for too long to
start slacking off now. Excellence isn't just a matter of
selling albums. Since he first laid eyes on soccer player
Ricardo Zamora, excellence has been a way of life.
Giving up on it now would not only end his career, it
would take much of the heart from his life.

Each recording session usually lasts for ten hours.

By way of comparison, the average Spanish singer cuts an album in fifteen less-intense days. But, as Julio says, "You can't make an LP with excellent sound quality in two weeks," and he vows never even to *try*.

Considering the enormous pressures Julio puts on himself—not only the long months he stays locked in the studio but also the level of excellence he sets for himself—it's all the more remarkable that Julio stays clear of drugs and excessive drink.

Although he admits that he once tried marijuana— "one puff, one headache"—he retains his childhood distaste for mind- or mood-altering stimuli. His rule of thumb regarding pills and drink is a simple one: if it's something that may not allow him to die "a complete old man" in mind and body, he says he doesn't want any part of it. The singer is perfectly content with his musical highs and, even if he's having a bad day at the studio or on the road, says he has too many responsibilities to surrender complete possession of his faculties.

"I know nothing of the snow that burns," he says of cocaine, "and I don't *want* to know anything about it." He rejects and to a great degree resents the comments of reporters and people in the industry that his extraordinary energy has to be derived from cocaine. Not only does he deny that he uses it, he takes pains to add, "And God grant I never need it."

Likewise, while he drinks more wine than he used to, he stays away from hard liquor and has never even come close to being drunk. "What for?" he asks. "I don't need it." If he has pain, he says he wants to remember it "because pain is part of the literature" of a artist. He adds, "Drink also makes you forget the happiness, and I certainly don't want to forget that."

*   *   *

After Julio put his most pressing recording obligations behind him, he was able to spend a bit more time
indulging in happiness. And one of the pursuits that
made him very happy was getting around to putting
down roots in Miami.

Julio already had several residences scattered around
the world, but none that he could call a real *home*. He
collected houses as a hobby, the way other people
collect stamps or coins. It was time to *make* a home, not
only for himself but also for his children when they
came to visit

And, as a new decade loomed, it was time to do
one thing more. It was time, Julio decided, to begin
planning that very tempting assault on the English-
language market.

CHAPTER NINETEEN

The house that Julio was to build himself was breathtaking. It did not come cheaply: before he was finished, he would spend a reported six million dollars raising his estate. That was almost as much as the combined totals of his homes in Madrid, Majorca, Tahiti, Argentina, and, later, in Los Angeles. But it's a showplace, and it suits Julio's personality and style perfectly.

The rolling estate is located in Indian Creek, an island off Miami Beach. Half the island is a golf course, while the rest is for homes: fewer than twenty houses in all, and most more opulent than Julio's, built like classical Southern mansions with large porches and stately columns. (However, Julio *does* have the largest yacht among the islanders, which he keeps anchored at a dock in his backyard on the shore of Biscayne Bay).

In light of the enormous wealth collected at Indian Creek, sole access by land is over a guarded bridge, with a police boat circling the island every fifteen minutes. The boat is frequently backed up by a helicopter, especially when private choppers, chartered by enterprising photographers, fly low over Julio's home.

It took Julio a while to obtain the property, which, when he first saw it, was owned by an old woman who was reluctant to leave her even older home. But money wasn't an object and he eventually got the property. Then, ensconced in a rented place nearby, he undertook a major face-lift of the land.

The first thing to go was the old house. Julio left a few walls standing, but not many: he wanted an open, Mediterranean look. While the house was taking shape, pool contractors were brought in to pour a pair of pools—one of which is always kept cold, the other warm—while landscapers reshaped the land to Julio's specifications. They also planted fully grown palms for, as Julio explains it, he doesn't have the patience to wait for small trees to grow. He wants to be able to enjoy them *now*.

The finished home has more window area than wall space, the sparse use of exterior stone and brick giving the house not only a sense of openness but also a feeling of exquisite delicacy. These qualities are reflected in the furnishings, which are low and do nothing to clutter the feeling of space inside. In selecting these furnishings, renowned designers Jaime Parlade and Mario Connio had only one restriction placed upon them: Julio said that in the living room, all of the chairs had to be big enough and soft enough so that if he felt like it, he could doze off in any one of them. While every chair in the room fills the bill, the sprawling silk pouf near the baby grand piano is sinfully inviting.

Julio can also fall asleep anywhere in his bedroom: in addition to the king-size bed, there are several plushly cushioned wicker seats including a huge, crescent-shaped wicker "throne" piled high with nine thick pillows. And if he *does* happen to fall asleep in the bedroom, Julio awakens to the sight of his expansive garden with the ocean lapping just beyond. Both are visible through the outside wall of the room, which is made of smoked glass.

The other rooms in his house—one each for his children, his mother (who lives with him and looks after the household while her son is away), the live-in help, and guests—are equally comfortable. Connected by white marble hallways, each room is thickly carpeted ("They seem deep enough to swallow swords," quipped Julio's visitor from *Architectural Digest*) and overflows with plants. Julio is determined to maintain the ambience of the Mediterranean, and greenery is an important part of that. So are the white-gloved waiters who constantly move about offering the lord and his retinue food, drink, and an occasional cigarette. The house is also stocked with all the latest electronic equipment, from videocassette players to projection TVs to cocktail table-style videogames (complete with customized seats).

However, while the inside of the house is intoxicating, the outside is where Julio lives. He can usually be found in one of the purple-cushioned chaise longues which surround both pools, each chair equipped with its own umbrella; if it happens to be raining, Julio still doesn't have to give up the fresh air, retiring to a large, Tahitian-style thatched cabana nestled in a corner of his property.

There's even an elegant doghouse to which Hey can retire, just in case the devoted pointer has had too much of the sun.

Julio has frequently speculated on his own mania for the sun, and has come to several conclusions. He has decided, first and foremost, that he not only gets his tan from the sun, but also his energy. "I drink from the sun," he says, "suck it up like a vampire. It's my battery." He doesn't care that too much sun can hurt him: his brother Carlos is a doctor—he gave up his career to move to Miami with his wife and three children and help manage Julio's career—and he's constantly scolding his sibling, reminding him that the sun can wrinkle his skin or cause cancer. But that doesn't deter Julio. In fact, he has begun wondering if it might not be possible to put a skylight in an airplane so that he can take advantage of all the time he spends traveling, and traveling so close to the sun, at that. Perhaps it's only natural that a star of Julio's magnitude would want to bask as much as possible in the biggest spotlight of them all. . . .

Julio also seems to feel a certain camaraderie with the sun. Both give light to others and, despite everything in their orbit, are very much alone—Julio notes that the sun's name is Sol, while he often feels that his own nickname is Solitude. He doesn't so much sit in the sun as commune with his soul mate.

The Miami sun apparently did more than warm his body. Once he was settled in, he began writing and recording some of his most ambitious works in years. One of them was a sequel to "Life Continues All the Same," but by far the most important song was his classic "De Niña a Mujer," "From a Girl to a Woman." For years, Chaveli had been asking her father why he had never written a song specifically for her, and the truth was he didn't know quite what to write. He has never been a composer who can contrive a song: "The magic arrives spontaneously," he says, "like a ray of light striking the white paper."

But one day, watching the statuesque ten-year-old during one of her vacation-time visits, he saw her differently than he had ever seen her before. She was no longer just the girl who wrote him notes from school when the teacher wasn't looking, or who asked him to send her postcards from around the world to add to her collection. She was now a young woman more than she was a little girl, and he marveled at the many ways in which those changes manifest themselves—physically, emotionally, and intellectually.

The "magic" which hit him took the form of a father's bittersweet reflections on those changes, and Julio's moving recording of the song gave him his biggest international hit to date. Predictably, not only was the song itself enormously popular, but it rocketed the 1982 album *De Niña a Mujer* to unprecedented sales heights, even for Julio. In Brazil alone he sold a staggering two million copies the first year, while the Japanese snapped up over a million albums in half that time. The figures for Japan are particularly astonishing given the fact that the album was recorded in Spanish.

The album's success was gratifying, of course, though Julio had some serious reservations about the notoriety it brought Chaveli. While she had always been in the spotlight by virtue of being the daughter of Julio Iglesias, the album made her a star in her own right. Not only was her picture on the album jacket—CBS used Julio's favorite photograph of his daughter and himself, the one he keeps on his nightstand—but hundreds of magazines came to photograph Chaveli, to ask her about the song, and to talk to her about her life with her mother and stepfather in Spain.

Julio had wrestled with the ways in which he knew the song would complicate her life. He was particularly concerned that by making her face so well-known, she might be easy for potential kidnappers to spot. That thought was always in the back of his mind, not only for Chaveli but also for the other members of his family. And not without good reason: before 1981 was finished, one of his loved ones would indeed be abducted and held for ransom.

But in the balmy safety of his Miami home, he concluded that the good which would come to Chaveli would outweigh the bad. For one thing, the young woman would feel enormous pride being the object of her father's most personal song. For another, like any budding teenager, she would be thrilled to go into a record store with her friends and see her face staring out from the racks. Finally, it would bring them closer together. Julio saw so little of his daughter that he felt the album would keep him on her mind and be a constant reminder of his love.

Then, too, Julio admits that it gave him great personal satisfaction to be able to give his daughter "a place of glory" like this. It was something few fathers could do for their children and, in spite of his reservations, he followed his heart and made Chaveli the world's sweetheart for a year.

Putting down roots in Miami worked wonders for Julio, not only because of Miami's various assets but also because he had his brother and mother near. With more control over his life and routine than ever before, Julio also had more time to reflect on his life, his success, and his fans. And he decided that with nearly half his life behind him, it was time to put some of his thoughts and experiences on paper, and also to set the record straight regarding a lot of the misinformation which had been printed about him.

The result of his labors was the book *Between Heaven and Hell*, which, while it's classified as an autobiography, is really nothing of the kind. It's actually a flavorful, objective, very moving 283-page confessional. What Julio did was to pick up a tape recorder in his free time and talk about anything that came to mind. If he happened to be petting Hey, he would talk about the dog and how it was his best friend, and wander from there into a reminiscence or two about Sydne Rome. The next day, he might throw off some thoughts about the political situation in Spain or his plan to one day write a love song to the telephone. Or he might talk about how much he loves animals with the exception of cats "and any animals that scratch," or how proud he is of the fact that all his teeth are his own, and that not one of them is capped.

Although Julio's mother and his longtime journalist-friend Tico Medina reviewed the text to plug in dates the author may have forgotten—though not *too* carefully since, in different places, the text cites both 1943 and 1944 as the year of Julio's birth—neither of them made a serious attempt to restructure or, for that matter, even *structure* the book. As a result, it's disjointed and frequently redundant.

However, for all its narrative and editorial flaws, *Between Heaven and Hell* nonetheless provides a remarkable insight into the mind of Julio Iglesias. As the title suggests, Julio spends a lot of time explaining how the good in his life has always been counterbalanced by the bad, how he unwittingly surrendered his privacy, his leisure, and even his very security for the enormous fame and success he has enjoyed. But he never whines and is never strident, and his stream-of-consciousness epic may well be the most forthright and honest book ever written by a celebrity.

Though the book may not have been for everyone, everyone bought it just the same when it was published in May of 1981. If nothing else, Julio's fans had to feel that the cover illustration was worth the price of purchase: on one side there's a photo of Julio looking radiant and angelic; on the other side, lit from below and clearly forcing out a powerful lyric, he looks as though he's suffering the torments of the damned. The photographs reach out to the lover and mother in every fan, and no doubt helped make *Between Heaven and Hell* the international best-seller it was (translated into many languages, it has yet to appear in English). In the first few months, over 145,000 copies were sold of the Spanish edition alone, a staggering total given the relatively small size of the book-buying public in Spain, South America, and Central America.

However, despite the book's success, Julio insists he'll never write a sequel. Not only doesn't he need the money (he accepted no advance for his literary debut) but he guarantees that when he's eighty years old, he'll be so busy wringing every last moment of enjoyment from life that there simply won't be *time* to take a cassette recorder in hand and pour his heart out.

Perhaps. But in 1984, Julio wrote a lengthy article for *¡Hola!*, and he has also expressed continuing dismay about articles which have misrepresented him to the public. For a man who is always looking toward each new conquest, a sequel not only seems likely, it seems inevitable.

Chapter Twenty

For all the good things that Julio enjoyed in 1981, the year did not pass without handing him a serious disaster, the most wrenching he had ever known. Julio had thought that he could never feel worse than when he and Isabel separated, but he was about to find out how wrong he was.

Late in December, Julio's father was kidnapped. The people who abducted him in Madrid were Basque terrorists, members of the militaristic right wing of the E.T.A., a separatist organization commited to the independence of the Basque region of Spain. No one knew the identities or whereabouts of the guerrillas; nothing was known about the criminals save that they were demanding a ransom of two million dollars for Dr. Iglesias's release.

Upon hearing the news from the Spanish police, Julio felt as if he'd been smacked hard in the gut. His body literally just *sunk*, his shoulders dropping as the wind was knocked from his chest. It was his worst nightmare made real, and he couldn't believe it.

Just a year before, John Lennon had been slain in New York. Upon hearing that news, Julio says, "I felt

cold, frozen like a rock." Not only had the former
Beatle been slain, but the man who did it had been an
admirer, had shot him dead while he smiled at his hero.
Julio had always feared that someone might one day try
to kill him—perhaps "a person who feels mistreated
because you didn't give the button off your shirt or send
an autograph. Or the old lover, or the man whose wife
has looked upon me with love and feels betrayed. Or
the crazed ones [that] collect everything about you
[and] grab you by the sleeve, by your hair, even pull at
your testicles."

Upon learning that his hair was selling for a hundred dollars a lock, Julio even feared that one day he
might be hunted down for his scalp, like a rhino for its
ivory.

Yet, he had never been paranoid about his own
personal safety. For though it concerned him, his greater
fear had always been that someone would try to strike
at him by harming someone he loved.

In this case, the terrorists hadn't chosen Dr. Iglesias
because of a personal vendetta against Julio. They took
him simply because he was convenient to nab, his
relationship to Julio guaranteed widespread publicity for
their cause, and Julio had the kind of ransom money
they were seeking. Nonetheless, it's reasonable to as-
sume that Julio still blamed himself in part for the
kidnapping, since he had only recently written in his
autobiography that he loved his father more than anyone else on earth—even more than Chaveli, due only
to the fact that the sixty-six-year-old had far less time
remaining to live. If he hadn't actually *invited* someone
to attack the elder Iglesias, he'd obviously shown the
terrorists the surest way to gain access to his bank
account.

While Julio prayed that what he'd written about his

father did not prove prophetic, an antiterrorist squad worked on the case in Spain. Individual agents went to their various sources in the field, while others searched in and around known terrorist hideouts. All the while Julio sat by the phone, often with Carlos, and jumped each time it rang. Snatching it up, he would wait with agony to hear whether the news was good or bad. Most of the time it was neither, simply a status report from the police or Interior Minister Juan José Rosón about the government's efforts to find Dr. Iglesias.

The days dragged on, the new year arriving with no change in the situation. And though Julio was touched by the support he received from friends and fans around the world, nothing could lessen the hopeless desperation he felt as each day came and went. Of course, he would gladly have given two million dollars to have his father back; he'd have given everything he owned for his father's return. But if he did that, could he be sure that his father would really be released? And if it became known that Julio had capitulated and paid a huge ransom, mightn't that invite other extremists to target him for future activities?

It was impossible to know what to do and, worse, he was unable to influence the outcome or contribute anything to the search. Being a mere spectator while the government agents did their job proved to be one of the most trying experiences of his life.

Finally, on the eighteenth day of the ordeal, the investigating team learned that Julio's father was being held in a house in Trasmoz, a remote village in the northeastern corner of the country.

After considering their options, a decision was made to go for broke and, in the predawn hours of January 17, 1982, the heavily armed agents assaulted the terrorist hideout. The result of the raid was the successful rescue of Dr. Iglesias and the arrest of his four captors. "Success," of course, is a relative term. Since the kidnapping, Julio's father has spent more time at Indian Creek, and usually travels with him on his tours. Whether in Trasmoz or Miami, Dr. Iglesias, like his son, will always be a prisoner of some kind.

Looking back on those awful days, all Julio will say is that "My father and my family and I have decided that this was an unfortunate incident, but that our family is not going to stand still because of it." It was a bold, forward-looking attitude, which, by that time, was something of an Iglesias hallmark.

Even if Julio's private life was sometimes maddening, professionally he had been spared the kind of hard falls and harsh criticism other top artists have traditionally endured. However, the honeymoon with the press was soon to end.

In the fall of 1981, before the horror of the kidnapping, Julio had begun to make his moves on the English-speaking market. He did this by recording his first-ever song to contain a few English lyrics, "Begin the Beguine." For several reasons, the song was released only in Great Britain. First, many Britons were already familiar with his music, having spent time in France and in the rest of Europe. Second, if the song flopped, it wouldn't have any impact on the U.S. market, which was his real goal. England was more or less a way to get his feet wet.

He needn't have worried. With a great deal of support from England's Radio 2, the song reached the number-one spot by December, selling over a half-million copies. Powered by the song's success, a companion album featuring "Begin the Beguine" and old cuts from Iglesias's foreign-language library reached the number-eight spot, selling over one hundred thousand copies. A second single, "Yours," was released in March of 1982 and was number three before the month was out. It sent the album climbing even higher, to number five.

Julio followed his record success in England with a concert tour in October of 1982. The tour carried him from Dublin to Coventry to Brighton to London, where, in October, he sold out five performances at the Royal Albert Hall. The latter feat was not only unprecedented but critics went out of their way to praise the technical aspects of Julio's concert. The hall's acoustics are abominable under most circumstances, but with a forty-piece orchestra—which included a thirteen-piece horn section—as well as three backup singers, they *should* have been disastrous. However, with their typical attention to detail, Julio and his people worked with the microphones and staging until the sound was near-perfect, a remarkable achievement.

The performances were also noteworthy in that, for the first time in Julio's career, his personal security nearly broke down. During one performance, the clutch of women trying to hand him flowers or other gifts proved too much for the regular roster to handle, and reinforcements had to be called in.

To coincide with the tour, Julio released his second album in England, *Amor*, which quickly went gold. Also accompanying this activity was a media campaign which had him on magazine covers, TV advertisements, and visits to soccer teams—an unusual move intended to capitalize on the singer's unlikely background as a soccer goalie.

In 1983, hard on the heels of these successes, Julio scored his third consecutive gold album in England with the release of *Julio*.

It had taken less than a year for Julio to make it big
in Great Britain. But that didn't make him as happy as
he thought it would. During his concerts, he had done
most of his chitchat with the audience in English, but it
was halting and not nearly as fluent as he would have
liked. What's more, much of what he had sold in
England was not in English.

Finally, the United Kingdom was part of Europe,
and it had a European mentality. In order to crack the
mainstream U.S. market, he would have to move quite
a bit farther from his roots. His songs would have to be
orchestrated in the lush, time-honored tradition of Frank
Sinatra rather than in the European and Spanish mode.
He would have to polish his English, since the mainstream audience would be far less tolerant of a heavy
Spanish accent than England had been. And he would
also have to do a lot in the way of public relations.

The U.S. is more hype-responsive than other
countries—which is understandable, given the vast number of artists trying to establish themselves here. This is
especially true in the music industry, where the heavy
metal of the Scorpions can well be vying for the same
dollar as country-music star Kenny Rogers, bubble-
gummers Duran Duran and Loverboy, mainstreamers
Barbra Streisand and Neil Diamond, and black artists
like Stevie Wonder and the Pointer Sisters. These
personalities, as well as others in their respective fields,
have all scored "crossover" hits—records which, while
fundamentally true to their roots, have widespread
appeal in the mainstream music marketplace. Julio
knew that he would somehow have to perform the same
feat: pick up the Johnny Mathis/Engelbert Humperdinck
romantic market while attracting the attention of other
consumers. Otherwise, he might end up with a cult
following like a 1980s Charles Aznavour, and that was

something he definitely didn't want. As ever, it was all or nothing for Julio Iglesias.

Finally, there was one thing more he would have to do to conquer the U.S. market—and that was the one concession which would earn him the greatest criticism from the Spanish-speaking critics. He would have to play to the Reagan-inspired nationalism which had captured the imagination of the country. Accustomed to being denigrated in so many foreign lands, Americans were going out of their way to embrace those foreigners who spoke of the U.S. with praise and affection.

To many Hispanic critics and fans, this was the equivalent of Uncle Tomism. But in fairness to Julio, prior to his arrival, the track record of Spanish artists in the U.S. mainstream had been abyssmal. Non-Hispanic Americans knew a little about some kinds of Latin music: Mexican mariachi; Afro-Cuban dances like the rhumba, the mambo, and the cha-cha; and the work of a few crossover artists like José Feliciano (who, though he was born in Puerto Rico, actually has lived in New York since he was five), Placido Domingo, and Xavier Cugat. They also knew about Desi Arnaz and his *I Love Lucy* band. Other than that mixed bag, the biggest names in Latin music meant nothing to the average American consumer.

Even today, long *after* Julio's first English album has shared a top spot on the charts alongside megastars like Prince, Bruce Springsteen, and Van Halen, Latin performers who cling to their heritage remain largely unknown in the U.S.—witness the relative obscurity of current Spanish-speaking superstars like José José, Roberto Carlos, Camilo Sesto, and even longtime headliner Raphael.

It can be argued that, if compromise were the alternative, Julio shouldn't have bothered with the U.S.

He certainly didn't need the money. At this point in his career, between concerts, albums, and various investments, his annual income was in the neighborhood of fifty million dollars. But he wanted the jewel in his crown and, besides, he fully intended to continue recording in Spanish and other languages. He believed—correctly so—that while a core of fans would be upset to be sharing their national treasure, the bulk of his fans would understand. As he himself summed it up, in a Spanish-language interview, "I'll still be singing ninety percent of my songs in Spanish, so I should at least *speak* in English for those people who do not understand our tongue." He concluded with the passionate appeal, "I implore you for a little assistance in this."

Rhetoric and controversy aside, however, the big question was not whether Julio should try to broaden his base. The question was whether he could possibly succeed.

CHAPTER TWENTY-ONE

J ulio was indeed *not* ignoring the rest of the world. He continued his output of foreign-language records and, though his triumph in England required a great deal of time and attention, he managed it concurrently with building his name in Brazil, a country which had never been an Iglesias stronghold. Using *"De Niña a Mujer"* as a launching pad, he scheduled a series of concerts in Rio de Janeiro and elsewhere and was soon the number-two recording artist in the country; by the end of 1983, he was selling three million albums a year. The only artist selling more records was Brazil's own Roberto Carlos; the fact that Carlos was also a CBS artist helped the label attract initial attention for Julio.

In Japan, Julio's track record was even more impressive: thanks to a tour there as well, his 1983 album *Momentos* became the country's most popular record, outselling *Variations* by Japan's own legendary Akina Nakamori by some fifteen percent. The only other non-Japanese artists within shouting distance of Julio were Simon and Garfunkel. And their widely touted reunion album *The Concert in Central Park* still sold over one hundred thousand fewer copies than *Momentos*.

In fact, *Momentos* topped most every other album in the world in 1982–3. It was number one in nearly one hundred countries, an international record, with the notable exception being the U.S. It was a smash on the Latin chart in the industry bible *Billboard*, but outside the Hispanic strongholds in New York, California, Florida, Texas, and Puerto Rico, mention of the singer's name brought an inevitable "Julio *who*?"

At the same time, Julio was sobered somewhat by CBS's inability to sell Roberto Carlos's English-language album to the U.S. market—though he felt that Carlos, being Brazilian, didn't have quite as much going for him as a European who could sing in six different languages. At least, Julio certainly *hoped* that that were true.

"Naturally I'm nervous about the future," he told *Billboard* while his U.S. battle plans were being mapped out. "I [must] come closer to the American sound, but I can't depart too much from what I've been doing." However, he said stubbornly, "it's the opportunity of my life, and I don't intend to fail."

He added that failure, in his view, would be his inability to draw ten thousand people to a concert in Ohio. As it turned out, less than a year after he established that criterion, nearly twenty thousand ticketholders would turn out to see him in Cleveland.

It is ironic that, as 1983 dawned and Julio was busy getting set to court America, back in Madrid, one of the oldest and most successful independent record companies in Spanish history, Discos Belter—the label of many of Julio's old favorites—was getting ready to fold. Julio didn't have anything to do with that, of course:

Discos Belter was dying because a foreign partner had pulled out of a long-standing relationship, and the Spanish company couldn't compete with the powerful multinational labels. Julio was simply emblematic of the problem: the marketplace in 1984 was a world marketplace, and only the multinationals survived.

To be sure, in the wake of Discos Belter's problems, the frustration the Hispanic community felt was understandable. And while it was only natural that some of that anger be directed at Julio, much of it was at once reactionary and overly harsh—as if, in expressing his delight with the U.S., he was ipso facto embracing it to the exclusion of all others.

For example, when Julio would later say to one largely non-Hispanic audience in New York, "I've just decided I want to die in America," that was obviously his way of thanking the U.S. for a particularly warm welcome. But one Hispanic reporter interpreted the remark as Julio sucking up to his audience by willfully distancing himself from his Latin supporters.

Another time, Julio was accused of being disrespectful of his less fortunate Spanish fans because he went on record as praising poor Americans for not feeling "offended because someone drives a Rolls," that is, not spitefully scratching the car with a knife or spitting at the owner.

It was painful to hear and read these things, especially when Julio had said over and over, in private and in talks with Hispanic reporters, that one of the things he hoped to accomplish in the U.S. was to open the door for other European artists. "I want to make a bridge between Latin music and American music that others can cross afterward," he had said.

But many of his detractors responded—and not without justification—that that was simply a side benefit. That the primary reason he wanted to succeed in the U.S. was to satisfy Julio Iglesias.

And so the resentment simmered, occasionally boiling over. But Julio has always said that while criticism, like exercise, hurts when he's in the midst of it, it inevitably makes him stronger. He says he was especially heartened by "the millions of human beings . . . you don't even know," the fans who sent him letters. He took to reading their letters while he had his breakfast each morning, and knowing that he had their love and prayers made his resolve that much stronger. He wasn't going to let a "militant" few make him miserable or change the direction of his career.

"I want to open those strong, heavy, difficult doors of America," he said. "It is what I wish above anything else in the world and [even] if I had to sacrifice my life in order to obtain it, I would do it without giving it a second thought."

One of the keys to the doors was not talent but publicity. To this end, Julio retained the public relations firm of Rogers and Cowan both to organize publicity and to counsel him as to what shows, benefits, and interviews he should and shouldn't give.

Rogers and Cowan is one of the most prestigious and powerful public relations companies in the world. Their musical clients include Paul McCartney, David Bowie, Olivia Newton-John, and Duran Duran, all of whom benefited enormously from the firm's expertise. Julio sat down with co-founder Warren Cowan and his associates late in 1982, and together they brainstormed as to how to introduce Julio to the U.S.

Cowan's objective was simply to "help a good product by making people aware of it," and he realized after his first two-hour meeting with Julio that he could begin a ground swell of media attention if he just put the singer together with some influential journalists. He was convinced that Julio would be "able to charm them and win them over, just because of his ability to transmit and relate. He has a lovely humility and is always kidding himself."

While they considered the best way to do that, it happened that actor Kirk Douglas and his wife, Anne, were looking for a major entertainer to headline their benefit for Technion, the Israel Institute of Technology. The fund-raiser was to be held at the Century Plaza Hotel in Beverly Hills in January of 1983, and not only would the press be there in force but the show would be aired nationwide.

Douglas recalls that he and the organizing committee "wanted to have some entertainment. And Anne—who is pretty good at these things—said, 'Look, why don't we have somebody different?' She's from Belgium and she said, 'You know, there's a guy who's well-known all over Europe but not very well known in the United States. And I think it'd be interesting if he would do it.'

"So," Douglas says with a shrug, "we asked him." Needless to say, Julio was delighted to be able to do it. Not only would the exposure be extraordinary, but he had a great deal of respect for Technion—which is Israel's equivalent to MIT. Israel had been very good to Julio: looking for music to provide instant relaxation from the many pressures they faced, Israelis made him one of their most popular artists. Indeed, in the wake of Julio and Argentine entertainer Mercedes Sosa, the most successful Israeli artists were those who took Spanish love songs and sang them in Hebrew. The Technion benefit would be Julio's way of thanking them for their support.

Since the fund-raiser was to be Julio's introduction

to the U.S. public, he wanted to do it right. He spent sixty thousand dollars out-of-pocket to hire fifty musicians and put on an extravagant stage show, and the results transcended even his most hopeful expectations.

Larry Vallon of the Universal Amphitheater in Los Angeles says, "Because the show was great, he became the darling of Beverly Hills society. He was in the society pages and every woman who was at the Technion benefit fell in love with the guy. What's more," says Vallon, "A lot of the people at the show were studio heads and record-company executives and really big opinion makers, and it all filtered down."

Recognizing a gift horse when they saw one, Rogers and Cowan jumped on the Technion bandwagon by putting together a "welcome to America" cocktail party for Julio at the fashionable Chasen's. Kirk and Anne Douglas were the hosts, and among the two hundred stars who came to the reception were Gregory Peck, Charlton Heston, Joan Collins, Andy Williams, and, prophetically, Priscilla Presley.

Naturally, the press was there as well, and nearly every major newspaper, magazine, and TV news show in the country carried a story about the Chasen's bash. Says Cowan, "It made him an instant name around the country. There was," he says, "almost an overnight awareness of Julio Iglesias." Kirk Douglas adds that he wasn't surprised at the extent and very upbeat nature of the coverage. "I think everybody who meets Julio likes him," he says. "He's a very gracious guy." Douglas is quick to point out, however, that all of the attention Julio received would have been worthless if he weren't as "talented and hardworking" as he is. Certainly the next few months would test both of those qualities to the utmost.

Having caught a tiger by the tail, the next order of

business for Julio and his associates was to get the singer on tour so that each important market in North America would get a close-up look at this living legend who had been unknown to them just a month before.

While the details were being ironed out—particularly the program, which couldn't ignore his Spanish, Italian, and French hits but had to include some English-language standards as well—Julio cleared the professional decks on his end so that he could spend more time with his language tutor. He'd been spending up to ten hours a day polishing his English, but he hadn't come as far as he wanted. Thus, he increased his schooling to fifteen hours a day. He wasn't trying to lose his accent, of course; as CBS East Coast marketing director Jeff Jones noted, "It adds to his charm and to the image of a Latin lover." But Julio did want to be as conversant as possible.

For its part, CBS supported Julio in the record stores by releasing "Julio," a compilation album of some of the international hits he'd be singing.

By the time the tour was set to kick off at New York's Radio City Music Hall on March 2, Julio was nervous but ready. The four-day engagement had sold out, helped along a few days before by Julio's appearance on *The Tonight Show* with a gushingly supportive Johnny Carson. Among the songs Julio had done on TV that night was the theme from *Gone with the Wind*, which was about as wholesomely American as one could get.

Julio needn't have worried about Radio City Music Hall—or any of his other engagements, for that matter. Backed by other TV appearances, which included *The Merv Griffin Show*, Julio sold out everywhere, including five dates at the cavernous Universal Amphitheater. He was also an unqualified success among the main-

stream press. While *The New York Times* noted of his
two-hour-and-twenty-minute concert that "he had yet
to achieve a comfortable fluency in English," they
emphasized that "his debonair charm and splendidly
virile singing made considerations of language almost
irrelevant." The newspaper added that Julio had
scrupulously avoided the "hammy histrionics [and] emotive overkill that male Latin singers often bring to such
material." In other words, he sang like an American.

The *Daily News* didn't dwell much on his music in
their review of his New York stay. "One look at Iglesias
tells you he's got a lot going for him," they panted.
"He's pure hunk, Latin sultry with teeth you need
sunglasses to look at." The tabloid did note, however,
that as far as singing went, his label as the Spanish
Sinatra was well deserved.

During his Los Angeles concerts three weeks later,
the formerly critical *Variety* not only praised Julio's
singing but also applauded the way he tried to win a
new following while going out of his way not to alienate
longtime fans. "It's a tricky situation," they wrote, "a
juggling act" which he handled by "singing in Spanish
(and Portuguese, French and Italian) as much as possible and speaking in English." They concluded that with
the addition of veteran U.S. producer Richard Perry to
his team, "Iglesias could make the transition to these
shores adeptly. He . . . really only needs the right reper-
toire to add the U.S. to his list of conquered countries."

Remarkable as it may seem, even after his triumphs
on the road during March, Julio still wasn't ready to
rush into an English-language album. The sales of his
Julio collection were strong, the album having gone
gold with over eight hundred fifty thousand copies sold.
But one comment which had surfaced constantly in the
press was that his audiences had consisted primarily of

older women. In other countries, where the market was less segmented and competitive, heavy numbers of men and young women were among his fans. But in the U.S., he was apparently being pigeonholed as a singer who appealed to the Perry Como–Dean Martin crowd. And Julio didn't want to limit his appeal to that devoted but comparatively small market.

During those first few months of 1983, one singer who was just beginning his rise to superstardom was Michael Jackson. And Jackson was doing it thanks to "The Girl Is Mine," a duet with longtime superstar Paul McCartney. Before that, Barbara Streisand and Neil Diamond had both revitalized sagging careers by teaming on "You Don't Bring Me Flowers." Even Johnny Mathis had made it onto the pop charts by cutting a pair of records with Deniece Williams.

Clearly, it was something Julio should look into. But who, what, and when had to wait. In April and May he'd be doing twenty-three concerts in Japan, and during the summer he was slated to tour Spain and Portugal. And he *did* want to be with his children when they came to visit during school vacation. Chaveli was enrolled at a boarding school in England, but Julio and Isabel both felt that it might be a good idea if Julio José and Enrique went to live with their father at Indian Creek. Not only would they be able to spend more time with Julio, but they would have their three cousins— Carlos's children—to play with. Only by spending time with the boys could Julio make sure that was something they really wanted.

He didn't even have time to consider director Roman Polanski's request that he take a part in a movie. Not only was he too busy, but movies held no fascination for him, especially after he saw the way that opera star Luciano Pavarotti had taken a critical pasting the year before in *Yes, Giorgio*.

But that was the middle of 1983. Two years later, when there were no more musical worlds left to vanquish, things would be considerably different. As those around him had come to realize, when Julio Iglesias says "No," what he's really saying is "Not now."

CHAPTER TWENTY-TWO

For most performers, the pressure of the work that Julio had left undone in the U.S. might have caused them to walk through the spring and summer engagements.

Even before he'd left Indian Creek for the Orient, CBS had announced that Julio's English-language album was virtually ready to roll—when, in fact, the songs had yet to be written. While the label was no doubt fearful that the momentum Julio had built up in the U.S. would cool, actually announcing the album months before he could possibly record it had to put a lot of pressure on the singer. And if the record itself didn't trouble him, he had to be smarting from the backlash which occasionally surfaced in the press as Julio's English-language debut became something of a Godot, infamous in its coming but never arriving.

However, Julio loves to perform, and as important as the U.S. was to him he refused to let anything distract him while he was in Japan. The Japanese certainly gave him every opportunity to strut his stuff, having snapped up over four hundred thousand tickets to the nearly two dozen concerts the day they went on sale.

Julio had always been big in Japan, of course, but CBS had expertly primed them for his visit. Several weeks before, the label had released five new albums consisting of library cuts, all of which received substantial airplay. At the same time, the eleven Iglesias albums available in Japan received prominent displays in every city where he was to appear, some stores going so far as to import albums from other countries to meet the unexpectedly heavy demand for new material.

Nor had Julio reached his saturation point. After the tour, in June, CBS released *Julio* in Japan, following it in October by a Japanese edition of what was arguably his finest album to date, the two-record *En Concierto*. Taped at performances in Japan, Australia, France, and the Royal Albert Hall, it not only served up all of Julio's greatest hits but captured the excitement, magic, and engaging stage patter of a concert.

Perhaps predictably, Julio's reception in Spain during his August tour was initially quite different from his welcome in the U.S. and in Japan. He wasn't returning a conquering hero but something of a turncoat. For days prior to his return, the Spanish press sniped at Julio for having been away for so long—both physically and spiritually—and Julio had no way of knowing what kind of reaction he would receive on the concert trail.

Fortunately, his first performance was a benefit at Palma de Mallorca, with King Juan Carlos and Queen Sophia among the concertgoers. The monarchs' presence was the equivalent of a big, wet "welcome home" kiss, and not only would it have been bad taste for the press to embarrass the king by continuing its broadsides against Julio, but the singer's grace-under-fire actually caused the critics to perform a remarkable about-face. Through his mammoth finale before over one hundred thousand screaming fans in Madrid's Bernabéu soccer

stadium on September 12, the media fell all over itself
to praise Spain's gift to the rest of the world.

However, when Julio tried to take his 127-person
troupe into neighboring Portugal, the sunny welcome-
home suddenly turned overcast. In an unprecedented
decision, the government refused to allow Julio to perform at Lisbon's Restelo Stadium. Officially, the Ministry
of Labor complained that promoter Alexandre Basto
had failed to obtain necessary official sanctions for the
concert. Basto dismissed this contention as nonsense,
since other concerts had gone through without a hitch
and Julio agreed, stating angrily that "there is no basis
for the nonauthorization of the show."

As it turns out, the contractual glitch appears to
have been simply the legal hook used to stop Basto
and Julio. The real problem was, apparently, left-wing
attacks on the government about the way people were
being allowed to spend their escudos on something so
frivolous when the economy was suffering from awesome inflation. Also, voices of protest were raised against
the government because so much foreign talent in
general was being imported (with the attendant expor-
tation of Portuguese coin) while so few Portuguese
artists were performing in other countries (and bringing
home foreign dollars).

So furious was Julio with the government's intran-
sigence that he canceled a concert he was to have given
on September 16 not far from Lisbon at Casino de
Estoril. It was a move which cost the Portuguese League
Against Cancer hundreds of thousands of dollars in
much-needed funds.

However, his mood was cheered somewhat on the
twenty-sixth of the month, when he was given a glittering
fortieth birthday party in Paris. There, Major Jacques
Chirac honored him with the Medal of Paris while *The*

Guinness Book of World Records presented him with
its first Diamond Disc award for having sold over one
hundred million albums around the world. Julio had
always appreciated the way the French had adopted
him as one of their own, and was deeply touched by the
gala celebration. He was delighted to be able to return
the favor the following spring by interrupting a hectic
schedule to attend a state dinner in Washington, D.C.,
in order to sing for President François Mitterrand.

Returning to the U.S. in October, Julio knuckled
down to the long-delayed matter of cutting his fifty-
sixth record album, his first in English.

Things hadn't cooled as badly as CBS appears to
have feared. *Julio* was now past the million-seller mark,
and Julio was still much in demand on shows like *The
Tonight Show* and *Good Morning America*.

Since much of the top writing, producing, and
instrumental talent in the U.S. record industry was
based in Los Angeles, it was clear that Southern California would have to become Julio's temporary head-
quarters. Renting a house at 1100 Bel Air Place in the
exclusive Bel Air section of town, Julio added songwrit-
er Albert Hammond to the key creative team of Ramón
Arcusa and Richard Perry. The selection of Hammond
proved to be critical.

To date, Hammond's biggest hit was "It Never
Rains in Southern California," which he'd both written
and performed nearly a decade before. Hammond had
learned Spanish as a youth growing up in Gibraltar, and
had also been friendly with Julio since they both met at
the Viña del Mar festival.

Perry says, "I brought Albert into the production
because of his musical abilities, and because his rapport
with Julio and his ability to speak both languages were

unique assets." Perry adds that that was extremely important because he had to find "songs that were both comfortable to Julio to sing phonetically [and] that he could relate to. The songs had to allow him to convey his style, yet at the same time be commercially appealing and acceptable to the American public as well as the rest of the world."

Not only would Hammond contribute some fine original songs to the album, including the all-important "To All the Girls I've Loved Before," but also excellent English translations of Julio's hits *"Me Va Me Va"* and "Bambou Medley."

It's fair to say that without "To All the Girls I've Loved Before," Julio wouldn't have ascended the pop heights to which he had aspired. The enormity of the song's popularity was not only unanticipated, but miraculous, given its history.

Hammond had written the tune back in 1976 with Hal David (Burt Bacharach's longtime collaborator). It was a good song, but it also had a rather arrogant, even chauvinistic slant as a man celebrated all the beautiful girls he has loved in his long, obviously active sex life. Still, they were hoping to persuade Frank Sinatra to record it.

But they were unable to get Ole Blue Eyes to give it a listen and, discouraged, Hammond put the song on the shelf. And there it sat until 1983, when one of the strangest collaborations in music history was hatched.

It came about when Julio stopped briefly in London toward the end of the summer. He was in his hotel room when he got a call from country-music superstar Willie Nelson. The country singer had heard "Begin the Beguine" on the radio and had called his label, CBS, to find out who this incredible Julio Iglesias was. When he learned that they shared the same record company, Willie obtained his number and immediately gave Julio a call.

"Hi," Willie said after introducing himself. "Julio, I'm here in London and I just heard one of your records on the radio. I think you're a great singer."

"Thank you," Julio replied graciously, repaying the compliment.

Willie continued, "The reason I'm calling is that I'd like to sing something with you."

This time, Julio was silent. Willie's suggestion flattered and astounded him, but at the same time he saw that it was the answer to the dilemma of finding someone with whom to sing a duet. Julio accepted at once, but there was a catch: Willie's schedule was such that they had to record it three days hence at his studio in Austin. Julio said that that would be no problem for him—which was true. It would, however, prove quite a problem for Hammond, who immediately went on a head-scratching search for an appropriate song.

"It seemed an impossible casting," Hammond recalls. "I mean, Willie and Julio. Where could you *possibly* find a song for them to sing together?"

From Julio's point of view, the more he thought about it, the less bizarre it all seemed. "Country is actually pretty close to Mediterranean," he believes, "mellow and melodic. If you take any Spanish or Italian melody and you put country backing behind it, this is country music." As an example, he cites Elvis Presley's "It's Now Or Never," which was derived from the classic Italian aria "O Sole Mio."

None of which helped Hammond on his quest, and after considering various songs written by himself and others, he began to wonder if "To All the Girls I've Loved Before" might not be suitable.

At first, he says, he was "afraid to suggest it"

because it was such an "unusual" song. But it certainly fit Julio's style (and reputation), and when Willie gave it his okay the singers decided to record it.

On the appointed day, Julio, Richard Perry, and their colleagues flew down. They taped the Hammond tune, managing to get it on just the third take—a record for Julio. Afterward, they all went out to dinner where they drank excellent Spanish wine that Julio had brought for the occasion. But they were all so high on the session that they decided not to let it end just yet. Instead, they returned to the studio and recorded a duet of "As Time Goes By" for one of Willie's upcoming albums.

Shortly before the record was released, Willie suggested to Julio that a good place to introduce it would be the nationally televised Country Music Awards. It would be a baptism of fire for the Spanish singer to perform on a country show, but he agreed; Deborah Miller, one of Julio's colleagues at the William Morris Agency, recalls, "It was a tough audience, and, boy, was he scared for that."

However, ever ready to rise to a challenge, Julio went on and, together, he and Willie knocked the audience out: by March, the recording of "To All the Girls I've Loved Before" was number one on both the pop and country charts. It ended up becoming the number-six single of the year, selling more copies than such widely touted hits as Tina Turner's "What's Love Got to Do with It," Culture Club's "Karma Chameleon," and Cyndi Lauper's "Girls Just Want to Have Fun." Julio even won a Country Music Association award and a Grammy nomination for his vocals, firsts in the country area for a Spanish artist!

Not that the song did only good for Julio. A lot of people in the industry found the teaming commercially contrived and utterly inappropriate. Mick Jagger laughed hysterically when asked by a *Rolling Stone* reporter what he thought of it ("Willie and *Julio!*" he roared. "That's a hilarious one!"), and *Esquire* condemned the duet, commenting that Willie was a genius who was wasting his talent on a "second-rate" singer. When other potential collaborations for Julio began to make the rounds in the record industry—team-ups with Diana Ross, the Beach Boys, legendary saxophonist Stan Getz, and the Pointer Sisters, among others—music critic Lynn Van Matre of the *Chicago Tribune* suggested that a good name for Julio's long-awaited album might be *Julio Iglesias Covers All Bases*, since he was obviously forgoing art for gimmickry, grandstanding in every area of music to court as wide an audience as possible.

These comments had to hurt the singer, even if Julio didn't necessarily disagree that he was using the duets to attract attention. In fact, Willie benefited as much if not more than Julio: overseas, where there had never been much of a market for Willie Nelson records, his albums became a hot commodity once "To All the Girls I've Loved Before" was released. In France, his annual sales jumped from 800 records to 60,000 albums; in Japan he sold 250,000 albums, and in South America more than twice that number.

But Julio wasn't about to make a point of that, and he had to face the fact that if influential writers and artists were coming to regard him as a joke, that could have a far-reaching and very damaging impact. Thus, except for the teaming with Diana Ross, he and his group downplayed the other duets which made it onto the finished album, "The Air That I Breathe" with the Beach Boys and "When I Fall in Love" with its fine tenor sax solo by Stan Getz.

The decision was simply to be Julio rather than the

ultimate crossover phenomenon he had apparently aspired to be. And while that may well have cost him some sales, it proved to be the best thing he could have done for his career.

CHAPTER TWENTY-THREE

Before Julio and his colleagues could do any serious collaborating on the new album, the singer found himself, as Willie would say, "On the road again. . . ."

First on the agenda was a twelve-show-a-week stay at the Celebrity Room of the MGM Grand in Las Vegas. Las Vegas, the stronghold of such romantic singers as Engelbert Humperdinck and Wayne Newton, welcomed Julio with enthusiasm: every show was a sellout and, though he stuck to his English-language palaver with the audience, it didn't matter which of his six tongues he used during the songs. As *Variety* observed, "He could sing 'em in Chad dialect, and the ladies would scream."

Following his stay at the Grand, Julio flew back to Los Angeles to tape "The All-Star Party for Frank Sinatra," then shuttled East to costar with Andy Williams, Leslie Uggams, and the Reagans in an NBC special called "Christmas in Washington." A few weeks later he was back in Washington, first to sing at the White House for the visiting Princess Grace, and then to entertain at the state dinner for President Mitterrand.

Julio also quite literally dropped what he was doing to fly to Mexico City to attend a dinner honoring Pedro Vargas, one of the grand old-timers of Mexican music. Julio never forgot how Pedro had helped him get a toehold in the Mexican market when he was first starting out, and he wanted to be part of any tribute to the legendary singer.

For all the pressure he was under, Julio was nonetheless in a good humor as he ran from engagement to engagement. One of the musicians who worked with him on the Los Angeles taping says that Julio "was very pleasant and ready to work. It was also my impression," he adds, "that Julio leads a very full sex life. There were a couple of girls at the studio, ushers, who climbed all over him. He seemed to enjoy that quite a bit, and had no trouble kissing and fondling them in front of everyone."

Despite the demands that Julio's schedule placed on his time, concentration, and energies, CBS still had hopes of getting an album out by the spring of 1984. However, those hopes evaporated when Julio got back to Southern California.

It was Julio's habit to record twenty to twenty-five songs for each album, from which he'd select the ten or twelve which turned out the best. In this case, however, he decided to record forty songs in order to get ten for the album. It was impossible for him to know, just looking at music or hearing recordings by other artists, what would work for him and what would not; he wanted the leeway to be supercritical and throw out more of his work than usual.

Given that it usually took Julio two or three months to record half that number of songs in a language with which he was comfortable, CBS had no choice but to push back the album yet again, this time to the fall.

(Whether the remainder of the songs he recorded is ever issued depends upon how Julio feels when he goes back and listens to them. A few which were too similar to cuts on the first album may appear on subsequent records; the others are likely to remain buried in the CBS vaults.)

On top of the sheer bulk of material he had to record, once Julio settled in for his two-month haul at the Sunset Sound studio, he discovered that his previous excursions into English-language songs hadn't quite prepared him for an album full of them.

For one thing, when he was on the road he had used "tricks" to get through English numbers. For instance, "As Time Goes By" from the movie *Casablanca* had been part of the program and, though his English was uneven, the electricity of a live performance minimized the errors. Or else he'd simply resorted to singing songs as bilingual duos—such as his standard "Embrace Me," which Julio sang in Italian while one of his backup singers performed in English.

Gimmicks and fudging simply weren't possible with vinyl. Repeated listenings would magnify each error, and he refused to use any vocals in which his pronunciation or intonation were less than perfect.

Then, too, as he broke in new material provided by Hammond and others, he discovered that it was more difficult than he'd imagined "to make the music and the words work together." He complains that "when the accent was good and correct, the music was often too fast" for him to *maintain* the accent. At other times, he simply found it extremely "difficult to get into the beat of the American music."

For example, Julio had never before recorded with drums playing so prominent a role in the rhythm section. Hammond says that it was necessary for Julio to learn to sing "with the instruments rather than just sing the song." That was quite an adjustment for someone who was accustomed to being backed by musicians, rather than "jamming" with them.

Slowly, however, he got the hang of it. And while he never matched the pace he'd set in the Criteria studio, he did pick up speed and confidence as the weeks passed.

One of the people who worked closely with Julio on the album was Tony Renis, an Italian singer / actor who had co-written both "De Niña a Mujer" and "Momentos" with Julio, as well as the international classic "Quando Quando Quando."

After one particularly grueling day, Renis noted, "Throughout my entire career, I never witnessed such a celebrity working nonstop" as Julio did on the album. At times, the effort left Julio physically and emotionally drained; more than once, Renis threw an arm around his shoulder and assured him that the results would justify the effort. In fact, Renis felt that something very important and very original was happening in the studio.

"Julio sings in English with an extraordinarily lyric, charming accent," Renis said. "The English language and Julio's voice form an incredibly fascinating blend; the former with special sounds not found in any of the Latin languages, and the latter with that unique phrasing and caressing of the notes which is [Julio's] trademark."

In order to help Julio feel at ease with English, the first fifteen cuts that he sweated over—including the Willie Nelson duet—were produced by Richard Perry. Once Julio and his associates got the hang of it, Perry turned the reins over to Ramón Arcusa, who produced the remaining twenty-five songs.

Interestingly enough, however, while he worked hard on the fifteen Perry cuts, when it came to making the final selections for the album, only three of the songs produced by Perry would end up on the finished record: "To All the Girls I've Loved Before," which was already a hit; "All of You," the duet with Diana Ross; and Hammond's "The Air That I Breathe," which not only had name value—it had been a smash for the Hollies back in 1974, when Julio's audience was listening to top-forty radio—but also offered the novelty of backup vocals by the Beach Boys. For all the hoopla about this album being Julio's first in English, the finished product would actually feature a great many songs with a Mediterranean / European sound.

Cynics have suggested that this was done to help create a taste in the U.S. for Julio's considerable library of non-English hits. Others have said that, according to CBS insiders, Julio's style simply didn't mesh as well with the more American tunes he recorded.

The truth is probably a combination of the two. However, it's ironic that after all the criticism he received from Hispanics, the finished album is not so much an American album as a Spanish album sung in English. Julio may have made compromises to succeed in the U.S. but, in the end, he was more or less true to his roots.

Meanwhile, during the first half of 1984, with his two duets climbing the charts in quick succession, his public relations people had no trouble keeping Julio in the public eye. In fact, their job was less one of drumming on logs than turning offers down.

The appearances which they did allow Julio to make were carefully contrived to expose without overexposing, to bring him to audiences that hadn't seen him to any great extent. While many media critics found this overly manipulative, it was a masterpiece of demographic targeting. As William Morris TV executive Deborah Miller explains, "We did 20/20 in April because of Barbara Walters and because it was a news-based story and exposed Julio to an audience he might not have otherwise been exposed to." Miller says Julio did the less prestigious *On Stage America* in April because that syndicated show brought him into homes in Middle America, where he had not yet toured widely.

Julio also appeared on the Grammy awards, presenting Melissa Manchester with the Song of the Year award, and made regular visits to *The Tonight Show*.

Indeed, an inspired visit to *The Tonight Show* not only garnered the kind of attention for which most publicists would sell their souls, but gave Julio an important insight into the minds of Americans.

During a show broadcast in June, Julio came out and announced to the audience that he'd just learned Willie Nelson was rehearsing down the hall and had agreed to come on and sing their duet. The audience went wild as, straight-faced, Julio asked them to welcome his dear friend Willie Nelson.

As the audience cheered and Julio applauded warmly, Willie walked out, as grizzled and leathery as ever. Only when the song began and the figure in pigtails, beard, and headband started to sing did the audience realize that Willie was really Johnny.

The duo managed to get through the song, though Julio wasn't able to keep a straight face beyond the first few bars. Whenever he wasn't singing, he was bent over with laughter or looking at Johnny with an expression that was somewhere between admiration and pity. For his part, Johnny didn't crack a smile the entire time he was onstage.

The outrageousness of the stunt not only garnered press but also did Julio an extremely important service.

Amid charges that he was as much hype as talent, it
enabled Julio to show his detractors that he could laugh
at himself. He realized that he could be *loose* in America, and that humanized him more than any interview
could have done.

Self-deprecating humor would thereafter be an
important part of his TV and stage persona, and the
timing could not have been better: not only was his
album in the wings but he was about to meet the
American public on a scale unprecedented in music
history.

CHAPTER TWENTY-FOUR

"**H**e seemed like a nice enough sort of man, but—why is he orange?"

Looking back on 1983–84, it's easy to forget that Julio's ascension was never a fait accompli. Although well-planned, well-financed, and brilliantly executed, his incursion into the English-speaking world had to overcome a great deal of ignorance and prejudice— witness the above quoted query from a teenage girl as reported in *The Village Voice*.

Even with all the attention he was receiving, no one was certain that come the fall his new album would surpass the sales racked up by *Julio*. And if, after all the expense, effort, and drumbeating, the new record did no better than old cuts from vaults, it would mean that the market for Julio was extremely limited. He would be regarded as a novelty, and that would be the end of Julio in America.

For that reason, it was both a blessing and a curse when Coca-Cola approached Julio back in November of 1983 with a proposition.

It was well-known that in March, Pepsi-Cola was preparing to launch a widely publicized series of TV commercials featuring superstar singer Michael Jackson. Ever since Jovan reaped vast rewards for sponsoring the Rolling Stones tour in 1981, companies had been keen to attach their name to that of a prominent singer or band. While nothing would be able to match the publicity generated by the burns Jackson received during the taping of one of the Pepsi spots, the company expected to sell a *lot* of soda and win the loyalty of countless consumers the following summer when they sponsored the "Victory" concert tour of Jackson and his brothers. What's more, Pepsi had singer Lionel Richie in the wings to do commercials aimed at an older audience.

All of which meant that not only was Pepsi well-positioned to reap a thick stack of publicity, they were poised to capture the attention of the minority market. Even if Coca-Cola had *wanted* to affiliate themselves with a black artist, anyone they could have selected in these pre-Prince and Tina Tuner days would have been a distant third in the popularity department.

Although no one expected Pepsi to knock out its competition with the one-two punch of Jackson and Richie, Coca-Cola was clearly obliged to do some grandstanding of its own during the summer.

After a great deal of brainstorming—drawing a lot upon the expertise of the Vail Group, a team of sponsorship experts based in Los Angeles—the soda maker began to feel that maybe Pepsi hadn't been so smart. While Michael Jackson's album *Thriller* was well on its way to becoming the top-selling record in history, many people inside the music industry and out regarded him as something of a fad, someone who would fade as fast as he'd risen. If that were true—as it turned out to be—Coca-Cola reasoned that the way to blunt the impact of Jackson and Richie was to hire a long-distance runner, one who was more class than flash.

Nor did he have to be black. If Coke could reinforce "purchase decision" in the Hispanic market, it would come close to counterbalancing whatever sales they lost among blacks.

Nor did he have to be under thirty. The target audience for Coke's products was the female, age eighteen to forty-nine, the one who did most of the buying for the home. Coincidentally, that was exactly the age group which bought the records of forty-year-old Julio Iglesias.

All of a sudden, Michael Jackson was looking more and more like a sequined white elephant. . . .

With crossed fingers, Coca-Cola went to Julio and suggested teaming on the most spectacular and expensive celebrity campaign in history. The proposal they made was threefold. First, Coca-Cola would send the singer on a thirty-city U.S. tour during the summer of 1984, with an additional thirty dates in Africa, Europe, and Australia spread out over the following two years. Second, they would feature Julio in a tasteful series of TV commercials which would air in one hundred fifty-five countries around the world. Julio would not be asked to sing a jingle the way Jackson had done, or overtly hawk the product; rather, he would promote Coke and new Diet Coke simply by having a can nearby and sipping it. Finally, Julio would represent Coca-Cola on important individual projects, such as the fund-raisers being planned to raise money for the refurbishing of the Statue of Liberty.

In order to mount the program, Coca-Cola was willing to lay out an unprecedented 8.5 million dollars—approximately $5.5 million for the tour and commercials, and the rest for Julio.

To say that Julio was overwhelmed is an understatement. However, as impressed as he was by the program, he asked for time to review it with his colleagues.

What CBS, Julio, and his advisors distilled from the proposal were two assets and two drawbacks. On the downside, Julio was slightly intimidated by the scope of the tour. He was in the midst of recording his album, and the last thing he wanted to do when he finished was to start hopping from city to city, holding press conferences and giving interviews in each. However, what appears to have been of greater concern was that the tie-in would give his detractors ammunition for their claims that he was selling the American public a packaged product and not an artist. He had become very sensitive to the issue, and also had to feel particularly wary about getting into bed with a corporate sponsor. Big corporations were under heavy fire for exploiting the Third World, and if Julio were to get caught up in that kind of controversy it could destroy his career.

However, Coca-Cola's reputation around the world was excellent, so there was no problem on that front. What's more, Coke was a long-lived and distinguished international product, qualities which Julio had always tried to project. Finally, there was no ignoring the sheer momentum the concerts would give his new album. The North American leg of the tour would last from June to September, the window during which his album would be hitting the stores.

Obviously concluding that no marriage was perfect, Julio realized that the good outweighed the bad and agreed to do the campaign. As William Morris officer Dick Alen observed, "He's going to be shown to two hundred million people all over the world, something no entertainer can afford to do by himself."

The announcement was made on May 2, at a crowded press conference held in the Astor Room of the Waldorf-Astoria Hotel in New York. Not surprisingly, there were moments when the entire affair seemed as contrived as Julio had to have feared. To wit, credibility was badly strained when Coca-Cola President Donald R. Keough said, "More than likely, while people around the world are listening to Julio, they are enjoying a bottle of Coke," and when Julio himself uneasily compared himself to a swig of Coke, stating that they both "appeal to the simple things in life—to a little moment of pleasure and refreshment during a hard day of work or a time of relaxation."

For the most part, however, no one was indelibly scarred, and the venture was off and running.

To the credit of the tour organizers, all of Julio's appearances were chosen with listener comfort and convenience in mind. For instance, while Julio could have filled New York's cavernous Madison Square Garden several times over, he was booked into Radio City Music Hall, where acoustics and comfort were superior. Not that he was being snooty: in Minnesota, he was booked into the Minnesota State Fair, while in other spots in the Midwest he would be playing outdoor stages where the audiences gathered on sprawling lawns for a very modest admission price.

After opening the tour auspiciously with a glittering United Nations benefit, Julio did two performances in San Juan, Puerto Rico, before flying to Denver—where he actually managed to one-up his own duet with Johnny Carson. After singing his opening song, he announced to the Red Rocks audience that Johnny Carson had stopped by en route to Wimbledon and

wanted to sing with him. Moments later, Johnny, once
again dressed as Willie, walked onstage. The audience
gave him a typically rowdy *Tonight Show* welcome, but
it died the moment he opened his mouth: this time it
really *was* Willie. The singer had been vacationing in
Colorado and had graciously agreed to come and help
Julio start his tour out properly. When they finished,
the cheers of the crowd chilled even the seasoned
veterans, Julio claiming that "It's a night I will remember all my life."

Not that the tour was all a bed of roses. *The New
York Times* reported that at Radio City Music Hall,
Diana Ross came to see the concert and even went up
on stage to greet Julio—but didn't sing with him "to the
crowd's audible disappointment." Instead, the video of
their duet was screened on a large-size TV, with even
Julio sitting that one out. The use of the videos for "All
of You" and "To All the Girls I've Loved Before" received unfavorable comment in many of the tour stops.

Many concertgoers who had seen Julio in their city
the previous year also noticed that he was sounding a
bit louder this time around. The fact is that the expense
of carting around a string section had been dropped
from the tour, the violins et al being replaced by
synthesizers. As *The New York Times* noted in their
review," "To compensate for the thinner musical texture, the singer's voice was echoed so heavily that it
occasionally lost its humanity and became an abstract-
sounding electronic instrument."

None of which prevented Julio from selling out
from Saratoga, New York, to Las Cruces, New Mexico,
and drawing a massive crowd at a spectacular Fourth of
July celebration in Washington, D.C., where he appeared
with the Beach Boys.

By the time the North American tour wound up

with a September 29 date at the Pacific Amphitheater in Costa Mesa, California, Julio had more than the successful conclusion of the tour to celebrate. His album had been released on August 13. The date had worried Julio, since he also happened to be staying in room number 13 in a Boston hotel on that date. But he needn't have feared any bad luck: one million copies were sold in just five days, and within a few weeks the album had reached the number-two spot on the charts. Entitled *1100 Bel Air Place* after his rented residence in Los Angeles, the record went on to exceed all sales expectations, selling over two million copies in less than half a year, dwarfing the performance of *Julio*.

Even his critics were running out of energy and epithets. As Spanish writer Juan Cueto grudgingly conceded—admittedly with a karate-chop pat on the back—"We have to recognize that it is no longer embarrassing to declare oneself publicly a fan of Iglesias. He projects a splendid sentimental vulgarity, without the slightest cultural pretension, with which we all identify for at least three minutes a day."

The world was truly his. Yet, that did not prevent Julio from moving forward to new conquests . . . as well as a few setbacks, including the two most humiliating experiences of his life.

CHAPTER TWENTY-FIVE

Between the North American and foreign swings Julio left his Mystère-Falcon 20 jet in dry dock and took a brief rest at Indian Creek. However, just *how* brief the rest was is made clear by the fact that, one afternoon, he got into the warm pool at the house and found it just *too* warm. Rather than go into the cold pool or wait for the thermostat to bring the temperature down, he called a local supplier and had five tons of ice trucked over and spilled into the pool. Even for the impatient Julio, this was a new height of indulgence.

The second leg of Julio's tour lasted from October of 1984 to February of 1985, and covered Europe, Africa, Asia, and South America. By the time he was through, he'd traveled over 90,000 kilometers, singing a total of 3,360 songs in 124 different stops.

No one bothered to calculate how much ice was melted in glasses of Coca-Cola during the tour. However, the first year of the campaign was an unqualified smash, surpassing even Coca-Cola's most optimistic projections. According to the trade newspaper *Advertising Age*, the company's sales increased a staggering one hundred percent in each of the key markets. Even more remarkable—miraculous, in fact—were the results of a contest which Coke ran in tandem with the tour. Called "Win a Magic Evening," the sweepstakes used point-of-sale registration blanks to enable a chosen few to win tickets to see Julio. Even allowing for ballot-box stuffers, Coke in no way anticipated the number of entries they collected: over 600 thousand in all.

For all the incredible records Julio set, and for all the wonderful memories the tour provided—his father had traveled with him and sat in the audience during every performance, making the tour especially memorable—it was not *all* sweetness and light. Press conferences had always been high on his list of dislikes, being "sterile" because they didn't allow for a good one-to-one with a journalist. Unfortunately, he had to hold over eighty of them on the road—and his manner occasionally grew rather testy, helped along by exhaustion as well as the brusque style of some reporters and their even more offensive questions. He wasn't surprised, just annoyed, that while he'd just spent hundreds of hours in the studio recording one of the most important albums of his career, most of the reporters insisted on asking him questions about his love life, his fortune, and politics. At one point, Julio became so miffed that he threw up his hands and demanded to know, "Why don't you ask the politicians questions about music?"

But the press conferences were a day at the beach compared to two nights which Julio wishes he could forget. One was the most embarrassing night of his life, while the other was simply the most depressing evening of his career.

The depressing night came first.

It was October 20, and Julio was in Frankfurt, West Germany. He was onstage and, early in the show, was getting ready to sing his hit song "Nathalie." As always at this point in the program, he walked over to the piano to sip some tea and honey. That night, however, the tea was cold and had been prepared with too much honey. As he drank it down, Julio says, "I felt something strange in my throat, and without even speaking I knew that I no longer had a voice."

Signaling for the orchestra to play, he left the stage, coughing softly as he gently tried to stimulate his throat. In the wings, he didn't try to speak but simply pointed to his throat. As aides clustered around him, he drank warm tea and honey and ate over half a loaf of bread. Julio claims, "I would have eaten fire if they'd have guaranteed I would regain my voice."

While he stood there, the orchestra stopped playing as the conductor came over to see what was the matter. Julio could hear the murmuring in the audience, and it was like a knife in his gut. His voice did not return, and he knew he wouldn't be going back. This was the first time since his postseparation depression that he would have to cancel a concert, and the first time *ever* that he'd have to cancel because of his voice.

One of his aides said that he would go and make an announcement, but Julio grabbed him by the arm and told him that he would go out himself.

Collecting himself so that he wouldn't be overcome by tears, Julio walked out as the conductor signaled for the musicians to leave their places. Standing beside the microphone, Julio watched as the orchestra members filed out, and when he was alone he looked into the audience. The houselights had been turned on and he could see the concertgoers; he hadn't counted on that, and braced himself for the sea of disappointed faces he'd be forced to endure.

"Ladies and gentlemen," he began in a dry, rasping voice, "I am very sorry to have to tell you that I cannot continue to sing. Something has happened, I don't know what—" He paused, choked with emotion, and had to swallow hard before continuing. "This is the first time in my life it has happened," he said, instinctively placing a hand on his heart, "and I apologize, deeply. All the money will be returned, and I thank you for having come. I only hope that we will be able to meet again."

He lingered a moment to give them the opportunity to react as they saw fit, and he was moved beyond words when the majority of the concertgoers reacted with understanding applause. He recalls, "A few of the women came forward and, smiling, placed bouquets on the stage. I went over and picked up everything." While he was doing that, Julio happened to look behind him and saw the instruments without the musicians. He cannot remember having felt more alone in his life.

Yet, of all the emotions he experienced while he was onstage, none was more painful than when someone shouted out, "It's a story! He doesn't want to sing!" Julio made no response, but says, "That was the saddest moment of the night, the one that did me the most harm. For those words, those intolerant words, were screamed at me in Spanish."

One of the constant problems Julio had to face, besides the rigors of the tour, was jet lag. Bad enough he had to fly from city to city every day or every other day and, landing at the airport, be carted off to a press conference or TV interview or working dinner with aides or journalists even before he had a chance to go to the hotel. Some nights he was so befuddled that no one, looking at him, would have reckoned him able to

remember his name, let alone answer yet another
question about his relationship with Priscilla Presley.

The zenith of Julio's disorientation occurred in
Antwerp, Belgium. He had landed in the city early in
the evening and, after making a TV appearance, went
to a dinner with the press which dragged on until two
A.M. Afterward, he met with close associates in his
room. During the meeting, Julio had stripped down to
his underwear in order to be as comfortable as possible.

The meeting ended at 3:30, at which time a whipped
and dragging Julio saw his last visitors to the door. He
watched as the elevator door opened and his guests
stepped in. "And as I stood in the hall waving good-
bye," he says, "the door of the room closed behind
me."

By that time the elevator had departed, and Julio
stood for a long moment staring stupidly at the golden
doorknob. After a moment he gave it a halfhearted twist
but, having stayed in literally thousands of hotel rooms
during his career, he was not surprised when it refused
to open.

Shaking his head, he glanced down the corridor.
There was a telephone beside the elevator and, with
rising spirits, he strode toward it, not daring to imagine
what he looked like dressed in this "irregular manner"
and hoping that no one came up in the elevator.

Dialing the front desk, Julio was unable to raise
anyone. Nor could he get anyone to answer at the other
posts he tried. Realizing that hotels in Antwerp must
shut down at ungodly hours like this, he looked back
down the hallway.

When he was on tour, key members of his staff
usually stayed in rooms near or adjoining his. Going to

the room next to his corner suite, he rapped on the door.

"About a minute later," says Julio, "a man of about sixty or seventy opened the door. Sadly, it wasn't a face with which I was familiar. Obviously he didn't recognize me, either, for, after looking at me very disgustedly, he said something in German and slammed the door."

Not wishing to take a chance at rousing anyone else and finding himself in a brawl, Julio decided that "there was no remedy but to go downstairs for the key."

Taking the elevator to the lobby and praying that it was deserted, he exited and walked briskly to the reception desk. There was a young woman on duty and, eyes widening slightly, she looked at the singer from top to bottom.

"Mr. Iglesias?" she inquired, as though wanting to make absolutely sure before she called the newspapers with the scoop.

Julio nodded once, smiling boyishly and wishing the earth would swallow him up.

"Well," she continued uncertainly, "is there some way that I may *help* you?"

"As a matter of fact," he responded, "there is. I would like the key to my room."

"Certainly, Mr. Iglesias. And what is your room number?"

Julio stared at her blankly and, after a moment, shook his head. "I'm sorry, I don't know. Is there some way you can check? There must be a record—"

"Of course." She smiled with excessive sweetness and, moving down the counter, began flipping through the standing file. Her fingers moved efficiently, but without the kind of urgency that Julio felt the situation merited.

After a few moments she had the room number, and turned to withdraw a duplicate key from his mail slot. As she did so, Julio felt a draft along the backs of his legs as a dozen or so people surged into the lobby.

Julio says, "It was a crowd of what looked like corporate executives who had gone out to dinner with their wives. They were all very elegantly dressed, and as they passed through the lobby toward the elevator, one by one their faces turned toward me." Worse than that, several of them stopped. And even worse still, one of the men walked over.

"Aren't you Julio Iglesias?" he asked, his eyes wide behind thick eyeglasses.

Two of the ladies cried at once, "Yes! Yes, that's Julio Iglesias!"

Julio recalls, "I made a timid gesture of acknowledgment and then turned back to the desk as though there were nothing out of the ordinary."

Much to his relief, the man with the eyeglasses rejoined his companions, the women giggling and the men drawing lewd conclusions as they entered the elevator.

"Thank God," Julio said under his breath as he heard the door shut behind him. Standing there alone, he looked into the young woman's eyes as they stood there, alone; her professional front had disappeared and her smile was more compassionate now.

"I don't know if it will make you feel any better," she said softly as she handed him his key, "but I have one of your cassettes in my car. I like it very much."

That she could be so sincere under such ludicrous circumstances touched the singer. And while he didn't linger, he did thank her warmly before scurrying across the lobby to put an end to what he has dubbed "the most ridiculous situation in my entire life."

...

CHAPTER TWENTY-SIX

The U.S. was good to Julio, and he knew it. At the end of 1984, just prior to leaving with his children for a vacation in Spain, he was asked by a TV reporter for one statement which would sum up how he felt at that moment. What Julio said was, "Thank you very much, America, for your hospitality."

Just how that "hospitality" translated into dollars is impressive indeed. Apart from the Coke monies, by March of 1985—a year after the release of "To All the Girls I've Loved Before," and just seven months after *1100 Bel Air Place* had hit the racks—Julio had already earned a total of $4.6 million from the record.

Interviewed by *Le Figaro* magazine in Paris in January of 1985, he repeated his gratitude, commenting, "It's beautiful to know that the Americans understood me and so quickly," he said. "That means a lot to me."

Both statements underscored the sensitive, emotive side of the artist. But there's another side, a more logical, pensive side which steps in and analyzes whatever his emotions have compelled him to say or do. "The conquest of America?" he told *Le Figaro*. "It's really very simple. One day you're on the Johnny Carson show, another day you're on the Merv Griffin show. Then you appear in five or six televised interviews and by then all Americans have seen you. The following week, at a store, someone runs across my record and buys it because it reminds them of something they enjoyed on the Johnny Carson show."

In truth, that's a somewhat smug simplification of American tastes. The Rogers and Cowan program got him exposure, but if the U.S. weren't ready to be serenaded, or if Julio weren't as good as he is, all the interviews in the world wouldn't have helped him.

But the two comments—the gratitude on one hand, the cool logic on the other—indicates the perpetual battle raging inside of Julio Iglesias, the conflict between instinct and intellect.

These two sides of Julio are currently wrestling for his attention as he contemplates his future. The big question he faces is what to do for an encore. After earning 680 gold records (signifying sales of 500,000 albums or more) and 221 platinum records (for sales exceeding one million albums), not to mention the Guinness Diamond record, numbers are more or less meaningless. He's already broken every music record in the world; all he can do now is put more distance between himself and his nearest competitors, Elvis and the Beatles—both of whom are no longer active. The problem with having this as a goal is that all the machinery is in place to see that it happens: all Julio has to do is cut the records and do the concerts. And that simply isn't enough for him.

"One gets tired knowing that you have everything safe," he concedes.

What new fields are there for Julio to sow? He's already gone the endorsement route in Europe, his likeness appearing on everything from perfume bottles

to eyeglasses to watches to—but of course—bedspreads.
Whether he'll allow that to happen in the U.S. depends
upon how the product reflects upon his image. Coke
was acceptable and, along with Melissa Manchester and
Kenny Rogers, he willingly sang "My music is on cable
TV" in promotional spots for MTV's video station VH-1,
which reaches the age 25 to 54 market. He is also introducing an elegant line of shoes for men and women,
footwear which he has personally designed. Presently
being marketed in Spain and Italy, the shoes will become available in the United States in the fall of 1986.
Prices will start at $60 for the women's shoes, $80 for
men's shoes. However, he is entering the field of commercial endorsements cautiously. The marketing of
Michael Jackson gloves, dolls, microphones, watches,
et al, contributed to Jackson's overexposure and fall
from grace, something which Julio will not allow for
himself.

Worldly possessions? In addition to his yacht, luxury cars, and homes, he has three corporations—two in
the Dutch Antilles, another in North America—to manage his holdings in land (which includes an entire island
in Polynesia as well as a sprawling farm in Argentina
which he's never had time to visit), apartment build-
ings, coffee plantations, and other kinds of real estate.
His Miami home is so personally and expensively
customized that, at forty-two, Julio Iglesias wants for
nothing in terms of comfort.

Vacations? He'll only go where the sun is shining,
and he's been to all those places countless times. He's
fond of night life and exclusive nightclubs and, when he
wants to unwind, heads for the Polynesian islands where
he can usually be counted upon to throw an extravagant
feast for everyone on the island. But that is nothing he
could do for more than a week or so at most.

Change his style just for the challenge of it? Not a chance. While he appreciates all kinds of music ("I love Boy George," he admits, adding with a smile, "in a *good* way, of course"), he has no desire to change. Not only does he enjoy what he's doing, but says he "learns and grows" each time he writes, records, or sings. Nor would his fans accept a radically different Julio. "Look at Fidel Castro," he says. "He's always dressed in fatigues, wearing a beard and smoking a cigar. Can you imagine him in any other outfit? I can change cars, an airline, but my style? Never!"

Marriage? Now *there's* a possibility. While he has reasons both to embrace and reject it, it seems likely that Julio will eventually become a husband for the second time.

He won't come right out and say it, of course. When Johnny Carson recently asked him if he'd remarry, Julio deadpanned, "Yes, why not—when *you* get married again, Johnny." To which Carson responded, predictably, "You're going to be lonely. . . "

The problem with marriage, Julio insists, is not getting married but living with each other "after." Still, more and more in interviews and conversation, Julio seems to be leaning in that direction.

Not that love is his primary motivation. He has been in love a great many times, most recently with a woman named Virginia, whom he refers to as La Flaca. Though he refuses to divulge her last name nor allows himself, as a rule, to be photographed with her, they have known each other for several years. Venezuelan by birth and Austrian by heritage, La Flaca frequently flies up from Venezuela to be Julio's houseguest in Miami and, says he, "Never has a woman looked into my eyes with as much love as she." Nor, he adds, does any "Miss Universe have as beautiful a body as she does." La

Flaca will stay in Miami even if Julio's away, tending
lovingly to his plants, taking in the sun on the deck of
the yacht—which is named La Flaca in her honor—and
waiting patiently for Julio to return so that she can help
him to relax.

While Julio has admitted "I love her," and that she
"has been the woman that has made me the most
intensely happy in the shortest period of time," he has
a tendency to reflect on personal matters to the same
excess he applies to each professional move. And that
makes marriage a problem. For one thing, he never
quite got over Isabel. As much as La Flaca loves him, it
was Isabel who "filled my life the longest time and has
given me three children." That they hurt each other is
irrelevant: what's important to Julio about any relationship is that it leave him with "a memory, full of colors
good and bad but *human*." Isabel did that, and a large
part of him clearly remains her devoted lover and
husband.

For another thing, as much as he loves La Flaca,
women on the whole continue to captivate Julio. He
says that sometimes he is "capable of maintaining three
women, loving them at the same time. Sometimes I
feel a bit Arabic . . . I like the game of love, two or three
women at the same time. I like to talk to them a long
time, look into their eyes, love them. I like them to
love me."

Yet, perhaps the factors which weigh most heavily
in Julio's mind are old age and loneliness. The older he
gets, the more he fears "old age, that day when my
battery runs low, when I can only give love in words."
And while he has countless friends, lovers, and associates, he still feels profoundly alone. His sons spend a
lot of time in school or with Carlos's children Tony,
Silvia, and Monica, and his beloved Chaveli has her

own life in England. Without them or a wife, he hasn't got the emotional anchor that has always given his life a purpose.

Those two concerns, powerful as they are, seem likely to team up and make a trip to the altar a very real possibility.

Nonetheless, Julio's artistic career remains his greatest passion, and satisfying it is his most immediate problem. There have been mutterings about Julio turning his talents next on the Communist countries. While he was on a concert swing through the Orient early in 1985, he went to China to perform, apparently testing the waters. His tendency has always been to go where no artist has gone before; however, government control of the media and the limited disposal income in Communist countries will not permit him to succeed to nearly the levels to which he is accustomed, and that may put him off.

More than likely, if Julio decides to tackle anything new on a large scale, it will be motion pictures. For years, he said he had no interest in the medium, since he considers himself "a very bad actor." What he does on stage is what comes naturally. Even if he were to study acting, he says, he doesn't think his fans would *accept* him as something other than Julio Iglesias.

However, after making two music videos for *1100 Bel Air Place*—"All of You" and "Moonlight Lady"—he has discovered that he's fascinated by what goes on "behind the camera." He says that becoming a movie director is a very real possibility for him and, early in 1985, preparatory to *some* kind of involvement in film, he made Los Angeles his principal residence in the U.S., moving his business offices there as well. If nothing else, he finds the weather "marvelous" and the creative environment stimulating.

In the meantime, Julio continues to study English, has completed a second English-language album, and is still recording in his other five languages. In April of 1985, he also proudly sang with fifty other Hispanic artists on the recording "*Cantaré Cantarás*," a record whose profits will go to feed the hungry of Africa and Latin América. (Ironically, the recording would not have been possible without a $150,000 grant from Coke's arch rival Pepsi-Cola.) Given his great body of work, it's not surprising that someone somewhere listens to a Julio Iglesias song every thirty seconds. Still, that leaves a half of every day to be filled with music and, knowing Julio, he'll find some way to fill it. Julio doesn't dismiss the thought, admitting that whatever restlessness he feels, he will never give up singing; that, musically, "there's a lot more that I want to give."

However, perhaps Julio's past and future both can best be summarized by the words he has chosen for his epitaph: "He stopped dreaming when dreams could be bought."

THE PRIVATE LIVES
BEHIND PUBLIC FACES

These biographies and autobiographies tell the personal stories of well-known figures, recounting the triumphs and tragedies of their public and private lives.

☐	25439	**JULIO IGLESIAS: An Unauthorized Biography** Jeff Rovin	$3.95
☐	24939	**JOAN COLLINS: An Unauthorized Biography** Jeff Rovin	$3.95
☐	34191	**CYNDI LAUPER SCRAPBOOK** Morreale, Mittlekauf	$4.95
☐	05102	**IACOCCA: An Autobiography** Lee Iacocca w/Wm. Novak (A Bantam Hardcover)	$19.95
☐	25045	**OUT ON A LIMB** Shirley MacLaine	$4.50
☐	25234	**"DON'T FALL OFF THE MOUNTAIN"** Shirley MacLaine	$4.50
☐	24511	**GIANT STEPS** Kareem Abdul Jabbar & Peter Knobler	$3.95
☐	24735	**CHANGING** Liv Ullman	$3.95
☐	23133	**'SCUSE ME WHILE I KISS THE SKY** David Henderson	$3.95
☐	25484	**AN UNFINISHED WOMAN** Lillian Hellman	$4.50
☐	25485	**DOVE** Graham & Gill	$3.50

Prices and availability subject to change without notice.

Buy them at your local bookstore or use this handy coupon for ordering:

Bantam Books, Inc., Dept. BG, 414 East Golf Road, Des Plaines, Ill. 60016

Please send me the books I have checked above. I am enclosing $_____
(please add $1.25 to cover postage and handling). Send check or money order
—no cash or C.O.D.'s please.

Mr/Mrs/Miss _____

Address_____

City_____ State/Zip_____

BG—8/85

Please allow four to six weeks for delivery. This offer expires 3/86.

We Deliver!
And So Do These Bestsellers.

SPECIAL MONEY SAVING OFFER

Now you can have an up-to-date listing of Bantam's hundreds of titles plus take advantage of our unique and exciting bonus book offer. A special offer which gives you the opportunity to purchase a Bantam book for only 50¢. Here's how!

By ordering any five books at the regular price per order, you can also choose any other single book listed (up to a $4.95 value) for just 50¢. Some restrictions do apply, but for further details why not send for Bantam's listing of titles today!

Just send us your name and address plus 50¢ to defray the postage and handling costs.

119 - 202 - 611